HOLDING
HER
CLOSE

HOLDING
HER
CLOSE

NEW YORK TIMES BESTSELLING AUTHOR
LEXI RYAN

DEDICATION

To Mira—for the chatty brainstorming sessions, for writing sprints, for Team Jake and Team Shut-Up-About-the-Jam, but mostly for understanding my neuroses in the way only a kindred spirit can. Thank you.

CHAPTER ONE

Janelle

THE HUSBAND-STEALING MEDIA WHORE on the screen tugs on her bottle-blond hair in a move that makes her look helpless and simultaneously thrusts out her breasts—breasts her husband bought her with *my* money. The camera zooms in on her face, then goes to a soft focus as her big blue eyes fill with tears. "We're stronger than this," she says. "Strong enough to weather any storm. But that doesn't mean it's easy. The truth is, Janelle Crane is obsessed with my husband, and some days I think she'll stop at nothing to get him back."

I fucking hate that lying bitch.

The television clicks off, and I spring out of my chair and spin around to see my twin brother with his arms folded across his chest, the remote gripped firmly

1

in his hand. "I didn't sleep with him."

Nate arches a brow. "I didn't think you did."

"I'm not obsessed with him."

"Didn't think you were."

I don't want Tom back. That's what I *should* say next, but I'm not sure those words are true. My ex-husband has always owned a piece of me. Since I don't lie to my twin but don't want to admit I'm not over the man who pulverized my heart, I don't go there at all. "Will you turn the TV back on, please?"

Nate frowns. "Why?"

"I need to know what she's saying about me."

"I disagree. What you need to do is ignore her. She's trash, Elle. Not worth your energy."

"I know. But I fucked up. Everyone knows I fucked up."

"Let it pass."

Shaking my head, I sink back into the chair and fold my legs under me. I'm at my brother's home in New Hope. Again. I'm a loser who has no life of her own. Because everything in LA reminds me of my failed marriage and empty life.

"No, she didn't!" my sister-in-law, Hanna, shouts from upstairs. Seconds later, she rushes down to the living room. "Did you see that?" she asks me.

I give my brother a pointed look. "Nope. Someone turned off the television before the interview was over."

Hanna frowns at her husband and snags the remote from his hand. "What's wrong with you?" She clicks the TV back to life and uses the wonders of modern technology to back the show up ninety seconds.

"Do you think your husband is still having an affair with his ex-wife?" the interviewer, Ina Turnstall, asks.

Bella flutters her lashes until a tear rolls out of each corner of her eyes. "I think he's only human, and can only be expected to turn her away so many times."

"I flipping *hate* that lying wench," Hanna growls, and I smile at the censored echo of my earlier thoughts. My life in LA may suck, but my life in New Hope is pretty fucking fantastic.

It's not your life, the devil on my shoulder reminds me, *it's your brother's.*

Nate scowls at the screen. "This is all his fault. If he hadn't asked you to dinner with him . . ."

If I hadn't gone . . .

Hanna looks like she wants to throw something. "You're going to take an interview to set the record straight on these accusations, aren't you?"

"What's the point? I got drunk, kissed my ex-husband, and got caught on film. This"—I wave toward the television—"is my punishment."

Last weekend, he invited me to dinner under the guise of a work opportunity, and then he fed me a story about his unhappy marriage. He said leaving me was the biggest mistake he'd ever made, and I believed him. I believed him when he told me his marriage was over. Then there had been more martinis and we finished our dinner and moved to a corner booth in the bar, and when the band started playing our song, my brain abandoned me, and I let him kiss me.

Fuck, who am I kidding? I kissed him back. Because he's Tom. He's the first man who ever made butterflies dance in my belly. The first man who ever made me come. My first love. My *husband.*

Or he was. Until he decided Bella was a better match for his sexual appetite.

My stomach clenches, and I wrap my arms around my middle.

My memory of our dinner is kind of sketchy after that kiss, but the pieces I retained include more martinis, laughter, and his hot mouth sweeping across my ear as he whispered all the things women want to hear. That I'm beautiful. That he never stopped loving me. That I've always been the one he thinks about when he closes his eyes at night.

I do remember the end of the night. I remember he asked to take me home and told me he didn't think he could breathe until he was inside me again. I refused. I said I wouldn't sleep with him until his divorce was final, and the words made me feel so noble. I wanted to take my piece of shit ex-husband home with me. I wanted to let him in my bed, and imagined that the next morning, we'd start planning our lives together, as if his years with Bella were nothing more than an unfortunate detour on our path to happily-ever-after. And I know how pathetic that sounds. But when someone leaves you while still in possession of your heart, you'd believe anything if you thought it meant they'd come back.

Now, I'm sickened by my own foolishness, and I have to cover my mouth.

"You can stay here as long as you need," Hanna says, her hand closing over my shoulder. "I mean that."

I've already been here all week, but if it were up to Hanna, I'd move in. "Thanks."

Nate clears his throat.

"Oh," Hanna says. "Right. I almost forgot. We're having a Halloween party tomorrow night. I hope that doesn't bother you."

People. Happiness. Ugh. "I'll hang at Brady's," I say. "No worries."

"We'd cancel it," Hanna says, "but we've already invited everyone. You should come. It's a superhero theme."

"Don't worry about me." I smile, but inside I wither. The last thing I want to do right now is go to a party and pretend to be happy. "It'll be a great distraction."

My phone rattles on the table next to me. When I see my agent's number on the display, my skin goes cold, goosebumps and all. "I'm going to take this in the other room." I sweep it off the table and answer as I head to the guest bedroom.

"Janelle!"

I cringe at the sound of Merriellen's high-pitched greeting. "Hi, Merriellen. How are you?"

"Fabulous. Listen, I just got a call from Helen, and she's thinking someone else might be a better choice for the role of Trista."

I squeeze my eyes shut. Any other film would be thrilled with my scandal—quietly, of course, but publicity is publicity. Helen Kerensky, however, is notorious for her eccentric conservatism. Since she insisted on including a morality clause in my contract, her reaction to this scandal shouldn't surprise me at all.

"I'm not having an affair with my ex-husband," I tell my agent. "That kiss was an anomaly. An accident."

"Sure it was, dear." I'm not sure if Merriellen doesn't believe me or doesn't care. Probably both. "You know I'm not interested in playing judge and jury to your personal life. I'm just the messenger here. You know how Helen is. She prefers to work with the . . . the more *wholesome* actors."

Wholesome actors. I should get a bonus just for not laughing at that oxymoron, but I don't so much as giggle, because this isn't funny. I really want this role. It's my chance to finally do a serious part in a film. Everyone in Hollywood has pigeonholed me since my days as an airhead on the sitcom *Roommates*, and this is my chance to prove myself. "Can you get them to hold off on making a decision? I really think this will blow over."

"I can try." Merriellen sighs. "This would be different if we could deflect. If you were seeing someone and could flash him in front of the press a bit."

"I am." *Oh my God.* It's like my mouth has a mind of its own. A liar-liar-pants-on-fire mind of its own. Seeing someone? No, I'm really not. In fact, it's been so long since I've had sex I'm not even sure I still remember how.

"*Really?*" She draws out the word, as if it's full of juicy innuendo. "Seeing someone or just sleeping with someone? You can be honest with me. Do you have a boy toy, Elle?"

"Not a boy toy!" *Oh, what a tangled web we weave.* "He's . . . It's kind of serious."

"You are? Who? How soon can you be seen with him?"

Oh fuck. What have I done? "Merriellen, I'm sorry. I'm at my brother's and he needs me. Can I call you back later?" *You know, once I've gotten my lies in order?*

"Of course. Good talk. Bye, hon."

"Good talk," I mutter as I end the call. I lean against the bedroom door and knock my head against it once, twice, three times. Then I take a deep breath, swallow my pride, and dial the phone.

"Well, if it isn't my Elly Belly," Matthew Hailey says when he answers. "I'm watching Bella's interview. I would say I was expecting your call, but I believe you said you'd *never* use my services."

Closing my eyes, I prepare to eat crow. "I was wrong."

"Well, take a deep breath, sweetheart, because we're gonna need to work fast."

* * *

Tonight, I meet my fake fiancé.

Those six words are enough to make bile climb up my throat, hot and sour. I'm pretty sure this is what hell tastes like. And I'm the one who put myself here.

Guests have been arriving for the last hour, but I've been hanging down by the river like a convict relishing her last moments of freedom. I put my hand on the door handle and take a final breath of fresh air. My world is about to change.

"Damn, girl!" someone calls behind me, giving me the excuse I need to delay my entrance into my brother's Halloween party.

Pulling my mask to the top of my head, I turn to see Krystal Thompson studying me, her hands propped on her hips. She's dressed like one of the characters from *X-Men* with a streak of white in her dark hair. I only know this because she told me that was her plan. Truthfully, despite my brother's best efforts, I don't know much about any comic book character who hasn't had a movie or two of his own. "Hey, Krys."

"Did you wake up this morning and think, 'Today, I will become every man's fantasy'? Because that getup is sexy as fuck."

I drop my gaze to my pleather costume—the heeled boots, skintight pants, and bustier that lifts my breasts to never-before-seen heights. Yeah. Not my choice. But the moment I hired Matthew Hailey to fix the clusterfuck I've made of my life was the moment I stopped getting to make my own decisions, right down to and including Halloween costumes, apparently. "It's a little much, isn't it?" The world already thinks I'm a skanky ho. I'm not sure how dressing like Catwoman is going to correct that problem, but Matthew is nothing if not thorough, and he insisted this was how I was to dress.

"It's perfect," she says. "And I'm jealous. I want to look that hot."

"You look hotter." I twirl my whip, but it falls

limply to the side. "*I* just look awkward."

She cocks her head. "So is it true? Your *boyfriend* is here?"

I swallow hard. This is just the beginning of the lies. I don't know how Matthew managed to start a rumor about me within my own group of friends in less than twenty-four hours, but that's pretty much his specialty. He insists that the best cover stories start at grassroots, which means no one but he and I know the truth. "He is," I say, trapping my squeaky voice in my throat before it can give me away.

"Who *is* he?" She turns to scan the cars in the drive, as if searching for a clue. "Hanna said that she and Nate didn't even know you were dating someone."

I shrug and offer my best mysterious smile. No, my brother didn't know. And neither did I. *Come on, Janelle. You're an* actress. *You can do this.*

"You ready?" Krystal asks, stepping past me and opening the door. "I don't know about you, but I need a *drink.*"

"Sounds like a plan." I follow her into the house and slide the mask on to cover my face. We go to the basement together, but when Krystal pushes into the crowd to greet people, I hang back.

The second-best thing about this ridiculous Halloween party is that no one knows who I am beneath this costume. Meaning no judgy pursed lips of the holier-than-thou; no sad eyes of those who love me and know what I'm going through.

But that's only the second-best thing. The first best is that tonight I will put an end to this nonsense about wanting my ex-husband. Or I better. God knows I'm paying Matthew Hailey a pretty penny to wave his magic media-twist wand over my life. I'm not exactly giddy with excitement, but I'm so ready to put this shit behind me. I hate lying to my family and friends, and I'm more than a little disgusted by the idea of making out with some hired stranger, but Matthew's edict echoes in my head.

We have to take control of the story, and that's never an easy task, but if you do everything exactly as I say, it will be a worthwhile one.

Taking a deep breath, I scan the party for the man who will be spending the next three months playing the part of my devoted boyfriend, and soon my fiancé. We were supposed to meet before the party, but his plane was delayed, so here I am, preparing to meet him in the middle of a crowd. When I spot him, I bite my lip hard.

Thank you, sweet Mary, mother of Jesus.

Matthew told me my fake fiancé would be wearing a Batman costume, but he didn't tell me how *well* he'd be wearing it. And, yeah, okay, it's a Batman costume, so I suppose he could be hiding a doughy middle under all that faux-Kevlar, but I don't think so. One look at his wide stance and broad shoulders and I just know this man is every bit as mouthwatering under the Batsuit as Christian Bale. And though that doesn't change how I feel about making out with a stranger, it does take a bit of the sting out of my fate.

My phone buzzes in my pocket, and I have to do a wiggle-bend contortion to get it out. It's a text from Matt, AKA Mr. Fix-It.

He's there. Are you ready?

Well, fuck, I'm not, but what choice do I have?

Can't I just introduce him to my friends and family like a normal person?

Stick to the plan, he replies.

There aren't even any journalists here. Nate is too protective of his family to let that happen. I promise to stick my tongue down his throat the second we're in front of a camera.

I know what he's going to say before I even get the text.

I thought you were an actress. Act.

Got it, I text.

I shove the phone back into my pocket and make my way to the bar, where I hope to find the courage I need to follow this plan. Public necking today, meet the family tomorrow.

The bartender is dressed as Supergirl and munching on a handful of raw carrots while eyeing the crowd.

I pretend to consider my options and stare at the row of liquor bottles behind the bar. Of course, I probably shouldn't drink at all, since I didn't eat all day, but there's no room for food in a stomach this packed with nerves. Vodka will help. There's *always* room for vodka. "Could you make me a lemon drop martini?"

Supergirl sighs heavily and swallows a mouthful of carrot. "You really want a martini glass on the dance floor?"

"Of course she doesn't," Krystal says, sidling up beside me. "Make it a lemon drop shot. Four of them, actually."

Supergirl nods in approval and mixes our shots.

"Four?" I ask Krystal as the bartender fills the shot glasses.

"Two of us with two hands each." She grins, shoots back her first, and makes a face. "Damn, that's sour."

Shrugging, I follow her lead. The sooner this alcohol hits my system, the better. I grimace at the taste but swallow fast, and Krystal and I take the second shot together.

"Better?" Krystal asks.

I nod.

"Have you two seen Asher Logan?" Supergirl asks. "I heard he was going to be here. Or Nate Crane? His wife hired me, but I haven't gotten to meet him."

"Oh, my brother should be around here somewhere." I pretend not to notice when she whips her head around to gape at me. I'm guessing she's about to piss her gossip-hungry pants. Nate and Asher are celebrities, sure, but considering they both live in New Hope and have children and wives they dote on, they aren't very interesting to the tabloid-loving portion of the population. "The key with Nate is to look for Hanna. If you find his wife, you know he's never too far away."

"You're . . ." She licks her lip but misses the chunk of carrot sitting there. Dropping her gaze, she slowly takes in my Catwoman costume. "You're Janelle Crane?"

I put a finger to my lips. "Shh. Don't tell."

"Of course," she says.

Yeah, right. I know her type. The only things she won't tell about tonight are the boring ones. Which is why I intend to be anything but boring. "I've gotta be incognito tonight so I can spend some time with my boyfriend in peace."

"Boyfriend?"

I put my hand to my mouth. "Could you forget I said that?" Her eyes light up, and I can see it now. Matt's right. Grassroots. This is the way to go.

"Who is he?"

"She won't tell," Krystal says. "But can you blame her with the way the media hounds her?"

I smile and lift a shoulder in a halfhearted shrug. "We're keeping it quiet." I walk away before the bartender or Krystal can reply. My work here is done. The bartender will be watching me like a hawk for the rest of the night, and soon enough talking to all her local friends about us. In a few days, Bella's story won't be dominating the news anymore. Mine will. "Now, if you ladies will excuse me."

Then I move toward the guy in the Batman costume, swallowing every bit of my trepidation and fear. More to convince myself than to play my part, I add a little sway to my hips as I stalk toward him.

Let's do this.

I grab his wrist to lead him to the dance floor.

"What the—" He swallows hard as he takes me in, his gaze eating me up from my stiletto boots to this ridiculously tight leather suit. From the way he lingers on my curves, you'd think he really was hot for me and not just some guy Matt paid to play the part. He lifts his dark gaze to mine and the knot of tension in my belly turns liquid.

Maybe this costume is going to my head, but there's *chemistry* between us. I feel like my cells actually purr in attraction. It's hard to believe I was dreading this thirty minutes ago. Stepping close, I loop my whip behind his neck.

"Hey there," he says.

I want to get this part over with. Once we give everyone at this party a little show, the gossip train will start running and we can get out of here and talk about what comes next. "Just shut up and make this look believable."

I crush my mouth to his. At the age of fifteen, I had my first fake kiss filming a made-for-television movie, and I've had hundreds since. I know how to make a fake kiss look like the hottest, most heartfelt thing you've ever seen.

Only . . .

He gasps softly, right against my lips, and then he cups my jaw with his hand and slants his mouth over mine, and even though this is exactly what he's supposed to do, even though Matt's too good to hire anyone who can't pull it off, it's not what I expect. It's my turn to gasp. The slide of his tongue against mine sends electric sparks through me, lighting nerve endings I'd thought died in the wreckage of my divorce-ravaged heart.

My pulse stutters and stumbles forward all at once. It's no longer racing as much as scrambling to catch up. This is how kisses should make you feel. Like you want to crawl into the kiss. Like it's too much and too little all at once and you can't decide if you want to back away and catch your breath or throw yourself into it and risk never coming back.

When I realize I've lost control—that I've stopped thinking about why we're doing this—I jerk away and our eyes lock. His gaze is dark and intense.

Who knew eyes could reveal so much when framed by a mask? I imagine my eyes hold much of what I see in his—heat, passion, confusion.

Suddenly, I need to see him, and I lift up his mask to reveal Cade Watts's face. My mind spins for a minute, like wheels trying to find traction on ice, as I run through explanations. Did Matt hire Cade? Why would Cade agree to this?

My mental wheels find traction and take me right to the intersection of disappointment and mortification. This is not some fiancé-for-hire flown in from LA; he's a local police officer I've lusted after more than a few times.

"Who are you?" he whispers.

I back away from the need that has my gut wrapped in its fist, and from the desire in Cade's eyes. I back away from the evidence that I, again, am responsible for fucking up my own life.

I stumble as I trip over someone's feet.

"Janelle?" the man behind me asks. "What are you doing?"

Spinning, I see Batman. Another Batman. The *right* Batman? Maybe. Probably the one I was supposed to kiss in front of everyone. The one who was hired by Matthew and who's on board with my plan. Suddenly, I can't do this anymore. I'm sick of turning the other cheek, sick of facing the world with my chin up when I want to hide in shame.

So I run.

I pray my fake fiancé will leave me alone and save our plans for another day. Tonight, God help me, the only man I want chasing after me is one who can make me forget the world like that kiss just did. The only man I want touching me is Cade Watts.

CHAPTER TWO

Cade

I FIND CATWOMAN in the backyard, an empty shot glass dangling from her fingers as she looks up at the stars. Before I can think about what I'm doing, I take the glass from her hand, set it down, and back her against the side of the house. Her eyes go wide and her lips part—those pink, perfect lips demand all my attention.

"Listen," she says. "I—"

I kiss her before she can say more. Hard and then soft, because *damn,* her mouth is sweet and her hands are already looping around my neck, her body pressing closer. Maybe part of me likes that I don't know who she is. Maybe part of me is sick of worrying about tomorrow and the next day, sick of trying to morph my life into what happiness is supposed to look like and missing the mark every time.

I break the kiss. "Is this what you wanted?"

"Yes. No . . ." She draws in a shaky breath. "I shouldn't have kissed you." Her voice is vaguely familiar, but I can't place it. She arches her back, pressing her chest against mine. "It was a mistake."

"Probably." I stroke my thumb along her jaw, relishing that bit of exposed skin. "Are you interested in making another one?"

"You don't even know who I am."

"Do I need to?" I want to argue with any objection that might make her run from me again, but all I can do is ask the question. The next move is hers.

And she takes it, kissing me again, murmuring, "This is crazy," against my lips even as her fingers slide into my hair and she presses so close I'd think she was trying to hide inside of me. Then it's just lips parting, and tongues touching, and the feel of her body against mine. My hands take a tour of her sides, from the curve of her hip to the swell of her breasts. She's petite, but not one of those women who's all bone and hard angles. This one is soft in all the right places, and I want to feel those curves bare under my hands.

When Catwoman breaks the kiss, she pulls back and looks around, as if trying to remember where we are. It takes a minute for me to remember myself, but we're in Nate Crane's backyard, his Halloween party rocking on the other side of the wall. Music floats out from inside, laced with the sound of the wind as it swirls around us, crackling its way through the trees' unshed leaves. The light from the stars and a three-quarter moon make this feel more like a fantasy than reality.

"Give me a second?" she asks.

"Take all the time you need."

Her smile is shaky, and I watch as she disappears into the house. When she comes back, she grabs my hand, and her skin against mine sends electric sparks up my arm.

"Come on."

I follow her around the front and down to a house on the opposite side of the road.

"Isn't this Asher Logan's house?" I ask, when she slides a key in the lock.

"His wife is a friend of mine." She opens the door and heads inside, but I stop, staring at her back as worry eats at my gut. She must realize I'm not behind her, because she turns back to me after a few steps. "I'm sorry. Is this weird? I just thought . . ." She worries her lower lip between her teeth.

Damn, that mouth . . .

For a moment I was actually worried that she might *be* Asher Logan's wife. I'm all for the spontaneous hookup tonight, but I don't fuck around with other men's women. My worry is short-lived, however, and dissolves as soon as I make myself process it. Maggie has red hair, and my Catwoman has dark hair peeking out behind that mask.

"Do you want—"

She doesn't get the chance to finish that sentence, because I push into the house and kick the door closed behind me. Then my mouth is on hers again. I can't resist those lips and wouldn't want to. There's something about her that has my gut tied up in knots, and the only thing that eases the tension is touching her, kissing her.

Ridiculous. You don't even know her.

She leads me up the stairs and opens the door to a bedroom with a king-size bed and French doors that look out onto a balcony and the river beyond. I'm vaguely aware of the house and the wealth evident all around me, but that fades into the background of my awareness of her. She moves like she was made for that costume, her hips swaying as she walks, the shiny black material showing off the perfect rounded ass beneath.

When she opens the balcony doors, fresh air and the rush of the river fill the room. She stands on the threshold—not outside or inside, as if she can't make a decision—and keeps her back to me. "Would you believe me if I told you I've never done anything like this before?"

I would. Another night, another woman, I'd probably think that was a bullshit line. But not with her. She's damn near fidgeting with nerves, and I want nothing more than to soothe them, to help her relax and forget whatever it is that has her simultaneously so desperate for and anxious about tonight.

"Neither have I." I come to stand behind her and wrap my arms around her waist before dropping my mouth to her neck.

"I'm not usually interested in one-night stands," she says. "But I need this. One night that's not about all the other bullshit."

"What's this about, then?"

"Attraction." She moans softly as I scrape my teeth over her earlobe. "Chemistry. Pleasure."

So that's what this is. Fair enough. This is better. This is what I need. She tilts her head farther to the side to allow my mouth better access to the sweet spot behind her ear. *What we both need.*

"You taste so sweet," I murmur against her neck. I tug her earlobe between my teeth again and suck until she moans. "I wonder if the rest of you is as sensitive as this spot here." My tongue darts out to touch the tender spot beneath her ear again.

"Why don't you find out?" She arches her back and the movement presses her ass against my groin thanks to the added height from her stiletto boots.

"Jesus," I hiss. I slide my hand down between her legs, cupping her then applying pressure there until she grinds her ass against my erection. "Where do I have permission to taste you?" I withdraw my hand from between her legs and she whimpers in protest. Spinning her around, I press her against the doorjamb and graze my knuckles over the exposed swell of her breasts. "Here?" I ask, and she moans her approval even before I drop my mouth to sample that sweet skin. I kiss each breast then open my mouth and slip my tongue just beneath the edge of the costume.

Her hands go to my hair, holding me and leading me and urging me on all at once. When I yank the top down and expose the peak of her breast to my mouth, her nails curl into the back of my neck.

I graze her nipple with my thumb. "You want me to taste you here." It's not a question, and she doesn't reply with words. She arches her back, lifting her breast to my mouth. I tease her, brushing my lips across her nipple and then my tongue. She returns my teasing with a hand against my cock. I can't stand the torment, and the sound of her moan as I draw her nipple between my teeth nearly undoes me.

She rubs me through my pants, and I wrap my hand around her wrist to pull her away. "You don't like that?" she asks.

"I like it too much, but I'm not done tasting you yet." I reach for her mask, wanting to see her face, but she shakes her head.

"Could we . . ." She cuts her gaze away from me. "I don't want to be myself tonight. You make me forget who I am." By the way she says it, I'm not sure if that's a good thing or a bad thing, but I understand that sentiment too well, so I nod.

"So the mask stays on."

"Yes, please."

"Then I'm going to need something from you."

"What's that?"

"I need more skin, precious. That getup is fucking hot, but it's in my way. You keep your mask on, but the rest of it needs to come off."

* * *

Janelle

Cade wants me naked.
Hoo-boy.

I step away from the heat of his body and his intoxicating touch, searching for a place where the air isn't so charged with crackling need.

This is insane. This isn't me.

But that's why I'm here, isn't it? That's why I want this so much. I don't want to be me anymore. Especially not tonight. I don't want to be the fool who kissed her ex. Who believed his lies. I want to be the woman in the mask who sneaks off with a man just because his kisses make her head spin.

I hold his gaze as I lower the zipper on my top, watching Cade closely as it falls to the floor. I'm not wearing a bra—there wasn't room or a need for one. He swallows hard, and his gaze drops to my breasts then lower, taking in my belly ring and the low waistband of the pants before returning to my breasts. My nipples are hard and aching, and every inch of me is on fire, despite the cool autumn air rushing in the open doors.

My hands shake as I remove the boots and then find the zipper on my pants and lower them slowly until I'm standing before him in nothing but this mask and a skimpy black lace thong.

"You're perfect," he says, his voice rough. He doesn't rush forward, but looks at me with so much *intensity* that every spot his eyes touch comes alive with a delicious tingling energy. "Lie on the bed."

My mouth opens with surprise, but the way he said it—the assuredness in the command, the confidence that I'd do whatever he asks—makes the muscles between my legs clench with need. Part of my brain warns this is too risky, that the night with Tom left me and my career on a dangerous precipice, and the wrong move will push me right over it. Tonight was supposed to be about fixing my mistakes and not about making more. But apparently it's the other part of my brain that controls my limbs, because I'm climbing on the bed, lying on my side so I can study him. Is there anything sexier than watching a man watch you?

Cade emanates this growly alpha authority, and that, paired with the greed in his gaze? *Mother, may I?*

"Roll to your back so I can look at you." He takes a step closer. The first one since before my striptease.

"You still have your costume on," I say.

He yanks his mask off his face and flings it across the room, where it lands with a soft *thunk*. "Better?"

I love that I can see his face without him demanding to see mine, that he respects my need for the mask even when I took the liberty to look under his at the party. He seems to understand how important my anonymity is to me. Could that be because he already knows who I am? Maybe. Do I want him to know?

My stomach squeezes and flutters all at once.

I shake my head, pushing that mess of emotions from my mind for another time. I drop my gaze to his costume. "Take off the suit, Batman."

He growls and takes a second step, his hands restless at his sides. "It's gonna cost you."

"Name your price."

"I want to know your sweet spots. I want to know how you like to be touched."

"Then come here and find out."

His third step brings him to the side of the bed, and

he skims his knuckles over one nipple then the other. "I want you to tell me. I want to hear you say it. Deal?"

"Deal," I say in almost a squeak. I can't imagine describing what gets me off, but it's even harder to imagine telling him no.

Cade removes the top half of his costume and stands before me in nothing but leather pants. He's all hard muscle with broad shoulders and narrow hips, just like I suspected before I knew who was under the mask. On his left shoulder, he has a tattoo of what I think is a Celtic symbol, and inked up his side are words in a language I can't make out. I wait for him to take off his pants, but instead he comes to the end of the bed, slides his hands under my hips, and tugs me to the edge.

I gasp even as my knees instinctively draw up, opening to him.

"Time to pay up," he says, settling his hands on either side of my hips and leaning over me.

I lick my lips and rise up onto my elbows. "You don't move like a man who needs to be told where to touch a woman."

The corner of his mouth tugs up into a lopsided grin. "Trying to get out of paying your debt?"

"Never. I'm a woman of my word. But you're not undressed yet."

"I don't have a condom, precious, and these pants will serve as a reminder of lines we won't be crossing tonight."

A condom. Right. Why didn't I think of that? Why didn't I ask Maggie where she kept hers when I got her key? But now that the line's been drawn in the sand, I can see it needs to be there. The condom is the obvious reason, but even if I had one, having sex tonight would complicate things—for me, if no one else. I was always an epic failure when it came to separating sex and emotions. But maybe tonight, beneath this mask, I can try.

Cade moves one hand to my breast and cups it before rolling a nipple between his fingers. "You like this?"

"Yes," I breathe.

He lowers his mouth and flicks his tongue. My nipples tingle, and I arch into his touch. His mouth latches on to me and sucks. He kisses his way down my belly as he sinks to his knees on the floor.

My breath catches at the sight of him there—his dark eyes studying the most private parts of me, his mouth a breath away from my sex. I'm not shocked by what he's about to do. I'm shocked that I *want* him to do it. Receiving oral sex has always seemed so much more intimate than intercourse. Intimate, but not particularly sexy or enjoyable. Tom is the only man I've ever let go down on me. I loved him, so it was special, but nothing I would have asked for even from my husband, let alone a near stranger. Right now I'm so turned on by the idea. There's nothing I want more than Cade's mouth on me.

He lifts his gaze to meet mine. "Can I taste you here?" The words are accompanied by his fingers trailing along the thin lace of my thong, and I shudder. Because it feels good. Because I'm tangled up with hot need. But mostly because by asking permission, he's snagged a piece of my heart in a night that's supposed to be about nothing but our bodies.

"Yes," I whisper, lifting my hips ever so slightly off the bed so he can remove my panties.

Instead of peeling away the lace, he cups my ass and lowers his mouth to my sex. Then his tongue is on me, stroking my clit through my panties, and I'm pretty sure he's a fucking genius, because the friction of the lace against my clit combined with the wet heat of his mouth sends me to the edge faster than anything any man has ever done to me.

He circles my clit then strokes it again, circles then strokes. I'm so wet and so swollen it's all I can do to keep my hips still. I bite my lip and focus hard on not grinding against his face, because I don't want to do anything that might make him stop.

And that's when he pulls away, and I want to whimper.

Tom used to do that. He'd put his hand between my legs and play with me just enough to get me excited, then demand a blow job or fuck me from behind with no concern for anyone's pleasure but his own. He really wasn't the greatest lover, come to think of it, but that wasn't why I married him.

I frown because Cade isn't switching positions. He's still kneeling between my legs as if he's waiting for something.

"Look at me," he murmurs. I don't want him to see the disappointment on my face, but I make myself meet his eyes. "You like this?" He brushes his knuckles over my swollen clit and another shudder rocks through me.

"Yes."

"And you like my mouth here." He slips a finger under the lace and circles my entrance.

"Please." I gasp. "I need . . ." I don't know how to finish that sentence or where to find the courage to try.

"You need my mouth?" he asks. "Or my fingers?" He slides one inside me and curls it, and I'm so close to coming, I clench tightly around him.

"Both," I manage. "I want both."

"Are you afraid to fuck my face, sweetheart? Because I feel you fighting it, and call me a selfish bastard, but I want *all* of you. I want you wild. I want you to move those hips and grind against me until you come against my mouth and around my fingers."

God, his words alone slingshot hot pleasure through me. I fight to open my eyes as he slides a second finger inside me, slowly fucking me with his hand and unraveling me from the inside out. "I'm close."

I'm treated to that boyish lopsided grin again. "Damn straight." He removes his hand from between my legs and repositions himself on the bed to kiss me full on the mouth. His kiss is long and slow and thorough, and I can taste myself on his lips. My abandoned sex aches as he peels my panties from my hips.

"Please." The word is barely a whisper. A breath trapped between our mouths.

He slides his fingers inside me again and rocks his palm against my clit. "I'll kiss you here again," he murmurs, his eyes locked on mine. "But promise you won't hold back on me. Squeeze my fingers. Fuck my face. Scream. Anything but holding back."

For the first time since he removed his, I remember I'm still wearing my mask. Right now I'm free to be anyone I want to be. And I want to be a woman whose lover tends to her needs and not just his own. "If you promise you won't stop before I'm done, I won't hold back a thing."

Just that quickly, he sinks to the floor again and his mouth is between my legs and his lips and tongue and fingers—*holy shit*—it's almost too much, and yet I rock into him because I want more. I crave it and the heady freedom of this night. *I need it.*

His lips wrap around my clit, and he sucks as his fingers curl to milk that sweet spot inside me. My hands fist into the sheets and I come apart, an orgasm that takes my whole body and wrings it out.

I definitely didn't fight it. And I might have screamed. But judging by the look on his face when he pulls us to the top of the bed, he's pleased.

"That was"—I draw in a ragged breath—"a first for me."

"Not your first orgasm," he says.

I release a puff of sound that would be laughter if I had any energy left. "No, my first orgasm from *that*." I shake my head lazily. "I'm not sure why I'm telling you. I just thought you should know."

He squeezes his eyes shut as if he's in pain and swallows hard. "Christ, you're sexy." He's not the first man to say that to me, but the way the words seem to scrape from his throat makes them feel more sincere than any compliment I've ever been given about my looks.

"Your turn next," I whisper, my eyes floating closed.

He chuckles. "Rest a minute. You earned it."

I obey, and he pulls me against him so my back is to his chest and his cock is cradled against my ass. I wriggle against his length and moan as I imagine what it'd be like to have a man like this inside me. Would he still be so selfless? So driven by my pleasure?

"Be still, woman," he growls against my ear. "I'm trying to be a gentleman here."

All that vodka followed by all that pleasure and my body is spent. I smile but don't bother to open my eyes. I just want a little rest.

* * *

I didn't mean to fall asleep, but I wake up to the sound of my phone buzzing. I reach for Cade, but it's not his arms around me anymore. It's the blankets.

I push out of bed and rub my eyes as I search for the light switch. I'm in the room alone. The clock on the bedside table reads three a.m. Beside it is a note with a phone number.

If you can't catch me with the Bat-Signal, try this.

I bite my lip. Maybe. Just maybe after I put this whole morality clause mess behind me, I *could* give Cade a call. Would he understand why it took me so long?

Pushing out of bed, I find my pants and pull my

phone from the pocket. I have a text message from Matt. *Crap.* He's probably pissed I ditched my fake fiancé tonight, but no one's going to know the difference. What's another day?

The text message says: *Call me NOW.*

I ignore it and pull my clothes on. I don't need a lecture from Matt right now. That can wait until tomorrow. All I want to do for the next five hours is climb into the bed in my brother's guestroom and dream about Officer Cade Watts.

CHAPTER THREE

Cade

I HAVEN'T WOKEN up feeling this good in weeks. I got out of bed at five and ran, like every morning, but this time I smiled with each step.

Maybe I don't owe this mood to my mystery woman. Maybe I needed a night where I let go for once.

No, I know she's responsible for the grin I can't get off my face. Every time I close my eyes, I think about the way she moaned when I got my mouth between her legs and how hard she came when she finally let go.

At this rate, I'm going to have to spend my whole day in a cold shower.

I wanted to bring her home with me. When she fell asleep in my arms, I wanted to take off her mask and see the woman beneath. But something held me back. Something told me it was better not to spoil what we'd had. So I left her the note, pressed a kiss to the wickedly smooth skin of her bare shoulder, and left.

I'm just getting back home from my run when my phone rings. *Catwoman?* She probably hasn't even gotten out of bed yet, but part of me still hopes I get to start my day by hearing her voice.

My caller ID tells me it's my sister. Ignoring my disappointment, I swipe to answer.

"Good morning, sis." I head to the sink and fill a glass of water.

"I thought you weren't going to do this again."

"Haven't we talked about you lecturing me before six a.m.?"

She snorts. "Don't change the subject. I'm very upset. And whatever. You've probably been up and have run ten miles by now."

I only did four, but I don't correct her. When Laure's pissed, she's not to be trifled with. "Tell me what I did wrong."

"Don't be a smartass. I'm only hurt because you didn't tell me."

"Tell you what?"

"You said no more actresses."

I set down my water and it sloshes out of the glass and onto the counter. I don't like reminders of Cara any time of day, let alone before my first cup of coffee. "What are you talking about?"

"You're going to play dumb with me? Well, you can't. Not now that it's all over the internet." My sister has never been terribly rational, and when she's upset about something, her ability to jump to nonsensical conclusions is nearly superhuman.

Looking at the ceiling, I exhale slowly and count backward from ten. *Ten . . . nine . . . eight . . .*

"I mean, you know she's sleeping with her ex-husband, right? It's all over the news. She wants him back. But apparently she's gotta break my brother's heart at the same time. God, I *really* thought you were done with actresses."

"What are you talking about?" I don't like the cold chunk of ice that's taken up residence in my gut.

"And you didn't even *warn* me. Nooo, I have to find out while skimming my gossip sites. Who do I see? My brother dressed as Batman with his hands all over Janelle freaking Crane."

Suddenly, that rock of ice in my stomach liquefies, and I sink to the floor, my smile drowning in the fucking obvious. Those eyes. I should have recognized those deep brown eyes, that perfect mouth. I should have known who I was touching. I hadn't wanted to see the truth.

Fuck.

"I'm worried she's no better than Cara," Laure says. "This smacks of too much déjà vu, ya know? And Cade, maybe I wouldn't care so much if you weren't still heartbroken from the *last* second-rate actress who screwed you over."

I don't think anyone would call Cara Fray a second-rate actress. But heartbroken? Fuck. I'm not even sure that word covers what Cara did to me. She didn't break my heart. She stole it, used it, and spat it out. She decimated me, and I allowed it to happen.

I won't make that mistake again.

* * *

Janelle

There's someone in my room. Someone who wants to die, because he's saying my name and shaking my shoulder, and there's no way I've slept more than a couple of hours.

"Go away, Nate," I growl at my brother. I tug the sheets over my head and roll to my stomach. "I'm hungover."

"I don't give a fuck."

"Ugh." I flip back over. Brothers can be such—

Yeah, only that's not my brother. Not by any stretch of the imagination is this scowling, scruffy, broad-shouldered sexual Jedi at the edge of my bed my brother. I swallow hard as I look into the dark eyes that kept me under their spell for the better part of last night. Hell, who am I kidding? Those hours with Cade Watts were the better part of my week. Month. *Year.*

Judging by the look in his eyes, I'd say the feeling isn't mutual, and he's not here looking for a repeat performance.

That's probably for the best, considering today I have to get serious about Operation Fake Fiancé. But still . . .

"Promise you won't hold back on me. Squeeze my fingers. Fuck my face. Scream. Anything but holding back."

Damn shame.

"You know who I am?" I ask, dragging a hand over my face.

"*Now* I do. What the fuck were you thinking?" He plops his phone on the bed, and I reluctantly order my eyes to stop studying the way his T-shirt stretches across his pecs. They happily shift to appreciate the way his jeans hang low on his hips.

"Speak," he demands, pointing to his phone.

"So bossy," I grumble. Something flicks across his gaze—a memory of how much I enjoyed his bossiness last night, perhaps?

Doing my best to push aside that and all other memories from the last twelve hours, I grab the phone so I can figure out what has him so pissed off.

When my brain clicks on enough to allow me to process the words and images on the screen in front of me, I feel like I'm free-falling—like someone stole the bed and the floor and my feet all out from under me. "No."

"Yes," he growls. "And let me tell you something, sweetheart. I don't know where you got the idea that I was the one to fix the mess you've made of your life, but you picked the wrong guy."

I shake my head and hold up a hand, scanning the article as quickly as I can before going back to the top to take in the details. First, there's a picture of Cade and me kissing on the dance floor at the party. The caption under the picture reads: *Actress Janelle Crane and local police officer experiment with cosplay at singer brother's Halloween party.*

"Experiment with cosplay? It was a costume party

and they're making us sound like a couple of freaks." I look up at Cade, his hands propped on his hips, that talented mouth drawn into a thin line.

Okay, he's not an ally in this conversation. I go back to reading.

Janelle Crane, recently embroiled in a bit of a she-said-she-said scandal with her ex-husband's new wife, may have more on the line than her reputation. In fact, sources close to the actress tell us that Crane has been seeing someone new, and hinted that things are getting serious, but have refused to give a name. Could her new beau be the former LA homicide detective Cade Watts, who recently moved to the sleepy town of New Hope, Indiana?

Watts's new city is also the home of singer/songwriter Nate Crane, Janelle Crane's twin brother. The officer and actress were caught doing some pretty heavy dance-floor groping. Other party attendees reported the couple sneaking away to celebrity neighbor Asher Logan's house for a little privacy . . . and maybe some role-playing? Only they know what really happened, but one thing is clear: It would be hard to argue now that Miss Crane is still hung up on her ex.

Beneath that are two more pictures, one of me talking to Krystal on the porch before the party, my mask tilted off my face, and another of me on the dance floor with Cade immediately after I took off his mask.

I try to keep scrolling, but there's no more, only links to similarly trashy articles about poor souls as idiotic as me.

I'm a little scared to make eye contact with Cade again. He's pissed. Definitely pissed. And who can blame him?

I hand back his phone and steady my gaze on his chest. "It wasn't supposed to happen like this."

"Which part?" he asks. "The part where I figure out who I got off last night or the part where I find out that you used me?"

I meet his glare with my own then push out of bed. He slides his gaze over me quickly, pausing where the hem of my T-shirt skims my bare thighs before jerking it back to my face. I wave my finger at him. "*You* were the one who said you didn't need to know who I was."

He throws up his hands and starts pacing. "I was speaking metaphorically."

"You were . . ." I shake my head. My thoughts are traveling in too many directions right now—every one like a freight train bearing down on me and demanding my focus. God, this really isn't the time to notice how long his powerful stride is, or how he only has to take three or four steps to go the length of this room before pacing in the opposite direction. Also not the time to focus on his big hands and remember how they felt wrapped around my hips. But *those* thoughts? While ill-timed, they're far preferable to the freight trains and realization that I've screwed up. Again. "I need to call Matthew."

He stops pacing right in front of me and turns. "Matthew Hailey?"

How does he know Matthew? "Yeah. He's . . . a friend. He's been helping me after all the crap with

Tom."

He's frozen, staring at me. "Déjà fucking vu," he mutters. "Let me guess. Matthew Hailey is the reason you kissed me at the party last night."

"Yes. No." I shake my head. "I thought you were someone else. I thought I was kissing my . . ." I stare at Cade, helpless. I'm not supposed to tell anyone the truth about Operation Fake Fiancé and my plans to fix my reputation. Cade already knows too much. And not enough. "Matt will help us figure this out. We'll fix it."

I reach out to touch his arm, and he yanks it away like I burned him. "I'm not interested in being a part of any more of Matthew's *fixing*. You're on your own, princess."

"Cade, please."

"Please, what?" He steps closer, and I have to crane my neck to look at him. "Want me to pretend to be your loving boyfriend?"

I open my mouth to deny that and then snap it shut when I realize that's exactly what I need from him. Operation Fake Fiancé can't exactly continue as planned now, can it? "I didn't mean for you to get caught up in this. You don't understand how complicated it is."

"Don't I? Let me guess. You think sucking face with some wholesome country boy will make the press forget your sins?"

Again, he's too close to the truth. "You don't know what it's like. Having every move judged. Scrutinized."

"You screwed around with a married man."

"He was *my* husband first!"

His lips twitch in amusement, but his eyes remain angry. "You're all the same."

"Who? What are you talking about?" I feel sick, my hangover and my anxiety swirling together viciously in my stomach. "Last night was a mistake. That's all."

"You can say that again," he says, and I flinch. "To think I believed all that shit you fed me, as if it was special to you. As if I was offering you something you hadn't had before. Congratulations. You're one hell of an *actress.*" He says it as if it's a dirty word, but his disgust at my career doesn't hurt nearly as much as the way he looks at me does. I'm lower than a piece of chewed gum stuck to the bottom of his shoe.

"You don't know anything about me. You barge in here with your assumptions and insults—"

"I'm not here to fight with you," he says.

"Then why are you here, Cade? I didn't know there were cameras on us last night. That article isn't my fault." I want him to leave so I can cry. So I can hide. "What do you *want* from me?"

"Nothing." His voice is sharp and rough, gravel abrading my tender heart. "I'm only here to let you know I'm not playing this game. You're working with Matthew, so you must want to fix your reputation. Go for it. But find another patsy." He turns on his heel and storms from the room, slamming the door behind him and rattling the walls.

My phone rings and my hands shake as I reach for it, and when I see the name on the screen, three words come to mind: *Fuck. Fuck. Fuck.*

It's Matt.

40

Focus on damage control. But I can't stop thinking about the way Cade looked at me. The way he said *actress,* as if the word was bitter on his tongue. I know it was only one night, but there was something between us, something more than his talented mouth and chemistry so intense I must be exaggerating it in my memory.

"Hello?" I answer, pressing my hand to my chest. My stupid heart, always butting in where it's not wanted.

"Good of you to return my call," Matthew says.

"I was busy."

"I saw that."

God, I don't want to deal with his know-it-all shit this morning. I don't much care for what Matthew Hailey does. I always believed myself above the media-manipulating scandal cover-up games he plays. I guess that's why they say what they do about pride. And look how far I've fallen.

"I didn't know there were any photographers there," I tell him. Last night wasn't about the media. It was about Matt's "grassroots" gossip campaign. But, hell, everyone has a camera on their phone now. "And we were both in costume. I didn't think anyone would know . . ." Yeah, I can't even finish that pathetic explanation. The truth is, I couldn't stomach what I set out to do last night. Sure, I started to, but kissing the wrong guy was a reality check—a reminder of just how much I hate playing the game—and Cade was my way out.

He was more than that. He was my escape from

reality. For the first time since my divorce, I really *wanted* someone other than my husband. I felt *alive* in Cade's arms the way I haven't . . . ever.

Matt draws in a deep breath. Probably smoking one of those electronic cigarettes. That man vapes like it's going out of style. "You fucked up," he says.

"I know. Everything kind of just spiraled out of control. All because I kissed the wrong guy."

"You can say that again."

I rub my temples and try to banish the image of Cade's disappointed eyes from my mind. "Tell me we can still fix this."

Matt grunts. "Not likely. Seriously, Elle. Cade fucking Watts? You couldn't have chosen worse. If I didn't know better, I would think you'd set out to deliberately sabotage our plans."

"I . . ." I frown. "Wait." That article said something about Cade being a former LA homicide detective, but that's a long way from the Hollywood elite Matt surrounds himself with. "You know Cade? He knew you, too. How is it possible you know each other?"

"*You told him you were working with me!*" It's not a question but an angry screech.

"It just came out."

"Fucking Christ, Elle. You want to play the bimbo ditz for the rest of your career? Go for it. But leave me out of it."

"This isn't my fault." I shake my head, not liking how often I've spoken those words lately, and hating that they feel like a lie. "Okay. It *is* my fault. Completely. But I don't understand who got our picture and who found out we snuck off together."

"I had eyes at the party." Matt sighs. "The bartender had media connections and was there looking for a story. She had a guy out front."

"Fuck, Matt. You said last night was just grassroots—family and friends, no media."

"And *you* said you'd do exactly as I instructed. You were supposed to be with the guy I sent, not whatever local piece of man meat you found handy. What a fucking mess. What were you even thinking?"

"I wasn't." And it was a relief. To spend a few hours *not* thinking. To make decisions that didn't have anything to do with Tom or my career. "How do you and Cade know each other?"

"We don't," he growls.

"Bullshit."

There's a long pause before he finally answers. "He was dating one of my clients. Cara Fray."

"Cade dated *Cara Fray*?" Holy shit. Cara and I both started in this business when we were teenagers, but she's had a huge career. I have the sitcom *Roommates* as my claim to fame, but nothing of any substance before or after. My career is stuck in a rut and Cara's is cruising at warp speed.

"Yeah. Cara let it draw out way too long. I think she liked playing the commoner with the police officer boyfriend. Or maybe she just liked the way he kissed her feet and completely fucking doted on her."

"Or maybe she liked *him*," I mutter.

Matt grunts. "Regardless, she let things go too far, carried it on longer than needed. Then eventually she got bored, and she told him the truth."

"The truth?"

"That their relationship was only a way for her to make the press forget about her scandal with the director of *House for Two*. That she'd gone through the entire relationship on my instruction." He releases a long-suffering sigh. "Telling him was a total fucking violation of my contract, but that's Cara for you. You help her and she pisses in your face the second she doesn't have a use for you anymore. Thankfully, Watts's not the type to flap his lips to the press."

"You had her *use* him? You're telling me he didn't know it wasn't real? That's horrible!"

Another grunt. "I'm sure unlimited access to her hot pussy was a serious hardship for him."

"You're an asshole." And I'm a bitch. Because Cade may have been a dick to me this morning, but now he's hurt again, and I can't stand that.

"Yeah, well, I'm the asshole you hired to fix your mess, but you fucked it up last night, and you fucked it up again this morning when you told him you were working with me. Jesus. You are one screw-up after another, Crane."

I can't deny that. But this screw-up started with something that seemed so harmless. I kissed the wrong man. A man I couldn't resist. A man who doesn't give a shit about repairing my reputation. A man who hates my guts because of who I am and what I do. If I knew Cade a little better, maybe I'd know how to fix this, but I only know him from my visits to town. He hangs out in the same social circle as my brother and his wife, but it's not like Cade and I have ever had so much as a single meaningful conversation. "How serious were things between him and Cara?"

"They were living together. He bought her a ring. That's when she told him the truth. After that, he left LA."

That more than explains the way he looked at me this morning. He wasn't seeing me. He was seeing the woman who'd betrayed him.

"How much does he like you?" Matt asks. "Any chance you can salvage this? Maybe spread your legs again and see if he'll play along?"

"You're disgusting."

"Irrelevant. Will he play?"

"No. He was just here. He's . . ." I swallow the self-pity that surges up in my throat. "He doesn't want anything to do with me."

"That's what I figured. Come back to LA. We'll need to get creative if we're going to fix this without Officer Watts's assistance."

Closing my eyes, I let myself remember Cade on the dance floor, how our kiss wrapped me in hope without warning. The way I felt at the first contact of our lips. A kiss from a stranger shouldn't feel like that. It shouldn't take your heart in its fist and light your nerves on fire. A kiss from a stranger shouldn't make you imagine the end of your loneliness is a breath away.

But Cade's kiss did.

Now he knows I'm working with Matthew, and he thinks I used him just like Cara did. It doesn't matter that I didn't. Even if I told him the truth, he'd still hate me for what I'm willing to do—the lies I'm willing to tell—to save my career. But without a family of my own, without a lover whose touch makes me believe in fairytales, my career is all I have. All I am.

Hope has always been a heartless tease.

"I'll be on the next plane," I say. I'm already packing my suitcase.

CHAPTER FOUR

Cade

W<small>HEN</small> I <small>LEAVE</small> J<small>ANELLE'S</small> <small>ROOM</small>, Hanna is standing in the hallway with her arms crossed and a scowl on her face. "You know, when I let you in my house this morning, I thought you were going to curl up in bed with her or whisper in her ear."

My jaw is too tight to smile. I try anyway, knowing it probably looks as sick and twisted as my gut feels. "I'm not in a cuddling mood."

"I wouldn't have let you in the door if I'd known you were going to yell at her."

"I didn't yell."

She arches a brow. "You didn't *whisper*."

"You could hear us?"

"Your *tone* was clear if your words weren't." She sighs heavily. "You know, she's been through a lot. When I saw you two dancing last night, I was *happy* you were the one she's been dating."

"Is that what she told you? That we're dating?"

Confusion flashes across Hanna's face, and I look away. If Janelle wants to lie to her family, that's on her. But she needs to be the one to tell them the truth and deal with the fallout. Not me.

"You have no idea what it's like to have someone you love betray you," Hanna says. She turns on her heel and walks away from me.

I step forward to stop her, then force myself back. What would I even say? That I know exactly what that's like? That I spend every day trying to forget?

* * *

Janelle

Bella is waiting for me. Bella of the fake tits and fake hair and fake sob story. Bella, who would have the world think I'm obsessed with her husband. Bella who slept with him when he was still *my* husband.

Calling today shitty is an insult to shitty days. If this is the price for the best orgasm of my life, I think I should consider a life of celibacy.

Bella's standing inside the front doors of my building in LA, looking at me like I'm some creature that crawled out from the sewer. Actually, I don't know how she's looking at me—she's wearing sunglasses as big as mine—but regarding me like a sewer creature is her MO, so I'm just assuming that's what's happening under those reflective lenses.

She, of course, looks stunning. A would-be Marilyn Monroe, if a less authentic one. She's injected and augmented in all the right places, and pulls off a little black dress in the middle of the day like a pro. I, on the other hand, look like shit. I have on a T-shirt and a pair of baggy jeans that are rolled at the ankles, and my hair is in a messy knot at the top of my head. I'm grateful for my oversized sunglasses, because I look even shittier with them off. I spent my flight having quite the pity party, and the party favors were mascara smears, bloodshot eyes, and a pounding headache. I feel like the Marilyn Manson to her Monroe.

"What are you doing here?" I look over my shoulder to make sure the doorman has closed the entrance. They only let in residents and invited guests—though that doesn't explain Bella—but that doesn't stop people from taking pictures from the street if given the opportunity.

Bella grimaces. "We need to talk."

I snort. Totally unladylike and completely ugly. The sound matches how I feel. "I'm pretty sure you already said everything you had to say. And you did it on national television, so kudos." I keep walking, trying to pretend her presence doesn't make me want to kick and scream like one of my nieces during a tantrum. How *dare* she come here?

"Welcome home, Miss Crane," the man at the front desk says. He hands me a stack of mail. "We've missed you."

My face feels stiff, but I force myself to return his smile. I've only been gone six days, and it's nice *someone* in this town wants me here. Even if he's just my doorman. "Thank you, Fred. Could you have my bags brought up from the car, please?"

"Of course. Is there anything else I can do for you today?"

I shake my head. "No. Thank you."

When I head to the elevator, Bella is on my heels. "Could you please talk to me like a mature adult?"

"Sure." Stopping, I turn to her and say, "Bella, you may go home now." I mentally add *bitch* instead of saying it out loud. See? I'm mature as fuck.

"This isn't about Tom," she says.

"I don't care what it's about."

"You are so selfish," she says under her breath, but loud enough so everyone in the corridor can hear. Then louder, she adds, "Your friend is in danger, and you don't even care."

A chill runs over me despite myself. It's not that I believe her. Bella will say anything to get what she wants. But what if she's telling the truth? "Who?"

She looks over her shoulder, eyeing Fred suspiciously. "We shouldn't do this here. We shouldn't be seen together."

No shit. After her interview, the gossip papers would love a picture of us together. I can just imagine the headline: *Bella Comer Confronts Her Husband's Mistress.* That wouldn't help my cause at all. But now I want to know what she has to say almost more than I want her to . . . No, I don't want her to drop dead. I'm not that violent. But I wouldn't object to her falling out of existence. As if the universe could just go *poof* and Bella never happened. Maybe then I'd still be married to Tom. Would we be happy? Or would he have found some other whore to screw?

I don't invite her up, but I also don't stop her when she follows me into the elevator.

The security guard stationed inside looks to Bella, and she shakes her head. "I'm going up to her place."

He turns his gaze on me and I shrug. "She's with me." I slide my card into the key slot and punch in for the penthouse. The security guard follows with his key to activate the elevator. I should really buy a house outside the city, but I'm in New Hope visiting my brother so often it seems pointless. Besides, this place has great security. Or so I thought, before they let Bella in the doors.

Rather than wallow in the awkward silence, I tear open the letter on the top of my stack and pull the paper from inside. "Get a clue," I mutter when I see it.

"What is it?" Bella grabs the letter from my hand—*rude*—and studies it. It's like the others. I've gotten at least half a dozen of these in the last month. Magazine clippings glued to paper to spell out, "She loves me. She loves me not." Daisies made out of construction paper adorn the corners.

When *Roommates* got big and I started getting substantial amounts of fan mail for the first time in my career, this stuff used to freak me out. I've gotten numb to it over the years. One thing you learn when you work in the public eye is that people are seriously freaks.

"Who sent you this?" Bella asks.

I shrug. "I don't know. Some crazy fan. I've been getting notes like that for a few weeks now."

She pulls off her sunglasses and settles them on top of her head. Her face is clean of makeup and her eyes are red and puffy. "Notes like *this*?" she asks. "You're sure?" Blood drains from her face.

"Are you okay, Bella?" What a ridiculous question to ask her, given what's going on between us. This whole conversation is ridiculous. Our sharing air in this elevator is ridiculous.

"Answer my question."

The elevator dings, and the doors slide open. We step into the foyer of my condo, and I reach for the letter, but she holds it from my grasp like a bully on a playground.

"What's wrong?" I ask. "Why's this different than half the weird fan mail Tom gets?"

Bella swallows and drops her gaze to the paper again. "Have you talked to Courtney or Jo lately?"

Courtney or Jo. The reminder makes the contents of my stomach curdle. This woman didn't just steal my husband, she stole my life—including my best friends. Courtney and Jo were my costars on *Roommates*, and my best friends in this city until Bella swooped in and stole them out from under me. I open my mouth to make some smartass comment about it when she lifts her eyes to mine and I see her panic. "I haven't seen them since the SAG Awards last winter." It hurts me to admit that, but not as much as it hurt to be around them and know Bella's a better fit for their lives than I am.

As much as I wanted to, I never *clicked* with them.

"They've been getting these too," Bella says, running her thumb over one of the daisies. "I had lunch with them last week. We were talking about weird things that happened with fans, and somehow Court and Jo put two and two together and realized they were getting the same notes." She holds the letter higher and turns it to me. Her hand shakes. "Jo had a picture of one of hers. It looked just like this."

"A *Roommates* fan, obviously," I say. "Why does this have you so freaked out?"

"Court was supposed to meet me for breakfast this morning, and she didn't show. She's not answering her phone either. I went to the police and they said they can't consider her missing yet."

Missing a social event isn't like Courtney at all, but everyone has off days. "You're sure you were supposed to meet her today?"

"Yes. Today. She wanted to talk to me about . . ." She drops her gaze to the floor and swallows. "I don't think she cared for my interview."

Something surges in my chest—the mini-triumph of knowing your friend is sticking up for you.

"I came here because I thought maybe you convinced her to ditch me." She stares at me for a long minute.

"She's not with me. Like I said, I haven't seen her for months."

"I *hoped* that she was with you. Because I believe she's missing. Like *for real* missing. Maybe it has something to do with those letters." She flicks her wrist and waves the paper. "These letters."

I fold my arms against the chills racing up my spine. I have to admit that maybe Bella was right to come here. "That's really creepy. Have you talked to Courtney's husband?"

"He's in Vegas. Hasn't talked to her since last night. He's coming home today to head in to talk to the police. In the meantime, Jo handed over the letters in case there's a connection and hired a security guard."

"Maybe she got trashed at some club last night and hasn't slept it off yet." At Bella's look, I shrug and say, "Or maybe something bad happened. We don't know yet." I take the letter back from her and lay the stack of mail on my entry table. "Thanks for letting me know. Please give me a call if you hear from her."

Bella stares at me for a beat, then she slides the sunglasses back onto her face, presses the button, and steps back into the elevator.

I'll have to give Jo a call and let her know I've been getting the letters too, but I'm not convinced there's a connection between them and Courtney missing breakfast this morning. This isn't the first time we've all gotten attention from the same nut job, and frankly, these letters aren't nearly as creepy as a lot of the others I've gotten. Even so, I'll take them to the police. Better safe than sorry, as they say.

First, I need a shower and a venti triple latte.

But my plans fizzle away when I walk into my bedroom. There on the bed are dozens of daisies with the petals removed and scattered around each stem. Above the headboard, written in red lipstick, are the words *Loves Me Not.*

* * *

Cade

"Is actress Janelle Crane having an affair with a married man? Or is her real passion for this hunky small-town cop?" the woman on the television above the bar asks. "All the details after this break."

Lizzy Bradshaw hops off her barstool, and throws a napkin at the screen and scowls. "I swear these gossip journalists have nothing better to do with their time than spread lies that ruin people's lives."

Sam, her husband, wraps his hand around her arm, tugs her into his side, and whispers something into her ear that makes her giggle, sigh, and then melt into him.

She looks to me. "Sorry about my outburst. I'm still a little bitter."

"Don't apologize to him," Hanna says from the other side of Sam. "I think he believes the crap they're saying about Elle." She lowers her voice. "I think he broke up with her this morning."

I clench my teeth. "Why do you assume there was anything to break?"

"We saw you two at the party last night," Liz says. "You two hid it well before, but once we saw you together, the truth was clear."

I have to shake my head. The naïveté of the people

in this town. I swear. "She's got you believing exactly what she wants you to believe."

"Are you saying my sister-in-law is lying to me?" Hanna says.

I shrug. "LA is a different world. You don't know what people are like there."

"Oh man," Sam says. "You didn't just say that."

"Janelle is a sweet girl," Hanna says. Her face turns red. "This is about what happened with Tom, isn't it?"

"He was my husband first." Fuck, I don't know if the woman is having an affair, and I don't much care, but she's clearly still hung up on the man.

"She kissed him and you're hurt," Hanna says.

"I'm *hurt*?" I take a deep breath and remind myself I'm not going to get involved in another Hollywood web of deception. But *fuck,* how long exactly has Janelle been telling people we were together? Who *does* that?

But I already know the answer to that question because I've been the schmuck before. Actresses will do whatever they have to if it means manipulating the media. It's like a game to them.

"How could you believe this crap they're saying about her?" Liz asks. "She didn't sleep with her ex."

"It was just one kiss," Hanna adds. "And I'm not saying you shouldn't be hurt—"

I hold up a hand. "Spare me, okay?" I turn back to the screen and the commercial for a Magic Mop.

"What did you say to her this morning?" The question comes from right by my ear, and I turn to see Hanna standing next to my stool. "What made Janelle catch the first plane out of here while there were still tears in her eyes?"

Sam clears his throat. If there's a universal guy code for "I'm not getting involved but I suggest you tread carefully," Sam's speaking it.

And I've officially had enough. Standing, I pull my wallet from my back pocket and throw some cash on the bar. "Have a nice night."

I'm halfway to my car when my phone rings. I'm not in the mood to talk, but the call is coming from the precinct in LA where I used to work, so I take it. "Watts speaking."

"Cade, it's Gormong. How are you?"

"Great. What's going on?"

Gormong releases a long breath. "Listen, she doesn't know I'm calling you, but your girlfriend's here at the precinct."

"My girlfriend?"

"Janelle Crane? I thought you might want to come out."

"Fuck," I mutter. Now she's telling my old friends we're together. I'm going to LA, all right. I'm going so I can strangle one infuriating actress and demand she put an end to this nonsense story before I have to do it myself.

"Yeah, sorry. I don't blame you for wanting to keep it quiet. My wife told me about you two, though. She saw it online and was pretty excited. Anyway, Janelle doesn't know I'm calling you, but I knew you'd want to know."

"Know what, exactly?" I don't bother trying to hide

the irritation in my voice.

There's a long pause, and when he speaks, his voice is low, as if he doesn't want anyone but me to hear what he's saying. "Someone's threatening her, Cade. Some fucker has been sending letters to all the girls from *Roommates,* one of whom is potentially missing as of this morning. In the meantime, someone broke into Janelle's condo. Judging by the flowers, we think that happened sometime yesterday afternoon or evening."

"Is she okay?" I don't want to care, but my stomach clenches despite myself.

"She's fine. He was gone when she got there, but he left evidence of his visit. He didn't damage anything. I think he was just trying to send a message. We're looking into it, but her building has the best security in town and still the perp got in. I didn't think you'd want her staying alone."

My stomach cramps hard as memories of Cara steal my breath. She may have hurt me, but I failed her when she needed me most. I can't fuck up like that again.

"Don't let her leave the station," I hear myself say. "I'm on my way."

CHAPTER FIVE

Janelle

I T'S FAIR TO SAY THAT I'M FREAKED way the fuck out.

They were just daisies. I don't know how many times I've told myself that. *Just daisies.* Harmless flowers picked apart the way they might be by a child, but they were on my bed, in my home, in a place no one but I am supposed to be able to access. And that message written over the headboard?

"Here. Drink this," someone says, and I look up. Tom shoves a cup of coffee into my hands. I haven't seen him since our ill-conceived dinner. He looks smaller, older maybe. He seemed so strong and handsome before, but now I can't help but compare his shoulders to Cade's broader ones, his voice to Cade's huskier one. "Venti triple latte," he says. "Thought you could use it."

"Is it spiked?" I ask, attempting a smile.

He looks around the police interview room—from the stark walls to the single table where I'm sitting. "It crossed my mind, but that might be frowned upon here."

"Thanks." He always was good at the little things—remembering how I take my coffee, what wine I prefer, and my favorite perfume. "What are you doing here?"

"I'm supposed to meet Bella. She's heading up the search party efforts for Courtney."

A chill runs through me, and then it's not a chill anymore. I'm shaking and I can't stop. Maybe it's lack of sleep. It's nearly six a.m. I've spent all night at the station, most of it in this same room where I gave my statement hours ago. The officer who interviewed me told me I could stay as long as I wanted, and I've taken him up on that. I'm nearly delirious with exhaustion, but I don't think even a week of sleep could calm my fried nerves.

Someone broke into my home and Courtney has officially been missing for twenty-four hours. The scene in my bedroom gave them reason to think there might be foul play, so the police have been handling her case as a possible abduction since I called yesterday. "What if he . . . What if I . . . Maybe if I'd been home Courtney would be . . ." My thoughts jump and scurry around like a frantic squirrel in traffic. Every direction brings me to a path I simply can't contemplate.

"Breathe, honey." Tom pulls out a chair and turns it to face me. He settles in and studies me. "Elle. *Breathe.*" He says my name softly, the way he used to when we were in bed together. As if I'm precious to him. As if I'm the best gift he's ever been given. I do as instructed, inhaling to the count of five and exhaling the same, repeating until the shaking subsides.

Part of my brain protests that Tom is the same lying cheater who broke my heart three years ago, but I can barely hear that part over the rest of my mind. I'm tired and scared and want nothing more than to curl into the arms of my husband—*ex*-husband. I can imagine what it would feel like so vividly it's almost painful. If he were allowed to comfort me, I'd rest my head on his shoulder and take a deep breath until my head was filled with his scent. If he were still my husband, I could pretend I was safe.

The door clicks and Officer Gormong enters the room. He looks as tired as I feel. "We found her," he says softly.

I straighten. "Courtney? Is she okay? Where was she? Did you find the guy sending the letters? Is there a connection?"

He clears his throat. "She's giving a statement now, but I can tell you we found her returning to her home, and she doesn't have any visible physical injuries."

"Her house? Where was she? Did she—" I stop when Gormong gives me a look. "May I see her after she's done?"

"Of course." He drags a hand through his hair, then his eyes ping-pong between Tom and me. "Everything okay in here?"

"Yeah," I say. "Better now that I know Courtney's safe."

Something crosses over his expression. "Well, I'm right outside if you need me." He gives a meaningful look to Tom before shooting me a final nod. He turns on his heel and leaves the room, pulling the door shut behind him.

Next to me, Tom exhales heavily. "Thank God." He lifts his eyes to mine. "You okay?"

"I feel like someone just hauled the elephant off my chest."

Courtney's safe. No. Gormong's face changed when I used the word *safe.* I'd guess he wouldn't choose that word. *No visible physical injuries.* That's a far cry from *safe,* isn't it?

"Janelle," Tom says. His eyes look sad. They really do. They're the eyes of an old dog stuck at the pound, one who's too afraid to let himself wish but can't help hoping. Or maybe that's just what I want to see, what I want to believe. Is it so awful when I'm this scared and alone to let myself imagine that my once-husband was telling the truth that night? Is it so wrong to wish the only man I've ever loved really meant it when he said leaving me was the biggest mistake of his life?

But I can't think about that now. I can't have Tom. So I push away those thoughts and focus on the only thing that matters. Courtney.

"They found her," I say. I need to hear those words out loud again and again. I didn't expect to say them so soon. I don't want to admit what I'd imagined we might be saying instead.

Tom takes my hand and squeezes it. I don't pull away. "This is so hard," he says.

"What's hard?" I study our joined hands.

"Sitting here when I want to hold you."

"Tom—"

"I know. I won't. I'll behave. But we never got to talk about what happened at the restaurant."

He's the same lying cheater, I remind myself. But I've always had one hell of a time with perspective when it came to this man. "There's nothing to talk about." I swallow and lift my chin. *Don't let him sweet-talk you.* "You lied to me and made me look like a fool."

"Just hear me out."

I pull my hand from his grasp. "Seriously? No way."

"Am I really so despicable that I don't deserve five minutes of your time to explain myself?"

"Not right now, and maybe not at all." Jesus. Does he realize what's happening here? He always did make everything about him.

"Don't shut me out. You don't have to go through this alone."

"Why? Because you're going to comfort me? Stand by my side and hold my hand?"

"I would." He sounds so sincere, but his eyes dart to the door. I guess he wants to make sure no one is listening to what he has to say. He's an idiot if he thinks there's no one on the other side of that glass watching everything that happens in here. I should care about that. I should bring it to his attention. But I stay silent.

"If only everything weren't so complicated right now," he says. "There's nowhere I'd rather be than by your side."

Don't believe him, I lecture my gullible heart. But it's hard to hear lies for what they are when you want them to be truth.

He glances to the empty doorway again before settling his gaze on me. "I miss you more than you could possibly understand."

I flinch. "Stop fucking with my heart."

"This is because of your police officer, isn't it? Because of the story you want everyone to believe?"

"What?"

He rubs the back of his neck. "I saw the pictures."

Shit. I've been so caught up in the break-in and Courtney's disappearance that I completely forgot I have another mess waiting for me. In the light of the last twenty-four hours, losing the part as Trista seems so trivial.

Tom's studying me. "The world might believe those pictures, but you forget that I know you better than that."

"Some days, I don't think you know me at all." I feel like I physically shrink when I say it. It's one of those truths I never dared utter during our marriage. It hurt too much to say it out loud.

"I know you, Elle. And I know you wouldn't have let me kiss you if there'd been anyone else in your life."

He's right about that, at least. "That kiss was a mistake."

Tom ignores me and continues. "And if things are so serious between you two, where is he now? No man who is serious about you would make you sit here alone. He's not the one that's here. *I* am. So either he's a piece of shit and doesn't know your worth when you're so obviously *way* out of his league, or . . ."

I fold my arms. "Or what?"

"Or the pictures were staged." He holds up a hand before I can reply. "I don't blame you for playing the game. I never meant to cost you the role. But don't pretend he means something to you when we both know—"

Tom jumps out of his seat as Bella walks in the door.

She's a beautiful mess, her makeup smudged lightly around her eyes, her long blond hair tied into a knot at the base of her neck. She's equal parts worried friend and beauty queen.

Tom rushes forward and wraps her in his arms, then presses a kiss to the top of her head.

"There's nowhere I'd rather be than by your side." But there he is. By *her* side, comforting her. Again. Always.

"They found her." Bella's voice shakes. "She's okay."

Tom strokes her back. "I know. The officer just told us."

Bella catches sight of me over Tom's shoulder and blanches. "Janelle," she says, stepping from Tom's embrace. "I'm surprised you're still here."

That makes two of us. But every time I try to leave, they have another set of questions for me and another reason I need to stay. I haven't pressed the issue because I'm scared enough to not want to leave the safety of this room. "I'm sure I'll be leaving soon, but I want to see Courtney first."

"Surely you're not staying at your condo," Tom says. "Where will you go?"

That's a good question. My stomach falls. I could

stay at my brother's empty house outside of town. He hasn't lived there since he moved in with Hanna, but the idea of being in that big place alone terrifies me. As for local friends, I don't talk to any of them enough anymore to ask any of them to let me stay.

"Who will you stay with?" Bella asks.

I'll have to find a hotel somewhere. *Alone.* My skin crawls. "I'll—"

"She'll stay with me."

I jerk my head around at the sound of the deep, familiar voice. Cade Watts strolls into the room. Hopping out of my chair, I open my mouth to say something—though I have no idea what—but before I can, he steps closer.

He slides a hand behind my neck and lowers his mouth to mine. "Hey, baby." Then he kisses me right there in front of my ex-husband and his trollop of a wife.

* * *

Cade

Janelle has the sweetest mouth, and I swear she must have magical powers, because no one smells this good after a night sitting in a police station.

I mean to kiss her hard and fast and then get her the hell out of here, but once our lips touch, my plans change. I want more, and I take it.

When I slant my mouth over hers, her hesitation lasts only a fraction of a second before she melts into me. Her hands slip around my neck, and she presses her body against mine, surrendering to me right there in front of her fucker of an ex.

Tom clears his throat, and I break the kiss and lean my forehead against hers. She keeps her eyes closed. I'm not sure if she's trying to steady her breathing or gather her thoughts or both. She looks so fragile—*feels* so fragile in my arms—and after what I just saw from the other side of the glass, it would be easy to tell myself that she's different than Cara. Different than everyone in this city.

"I got here as quickly as I could," I say.

I flew in on a redeye and spent the entire cab ride to the station on my cell making arrangements. When I arrived, I came in through the back and had Gormong debrief me first thing. I needed details before Janelle could object to me getting involved. Not that I expect her to argue. In fact, having some psycho obsessed with her right now works nicely with her plans. Looks like she found the perfect way to get me on board with lying about our relationship to the world.

Tom clears his throat again, trying to remind me he's there. As if I could fucking forget. I came to LA with a lot of doubts—about this case, about Janelle, and about my decision to jump in the middle of this mess. But if I had *any* doubts that Tom Comer was a selfish, manipulative son-of-a-bitch, the last ten minutes obliterated them.

"Stop fucking with my heart."

I stood on the other side of the one-way glass and listened as he told her he wished he could hold her. I listened to his theories about the pictures from the costume party. And then I stood there and watched as Tom shifted all of his attention from Janelle to his new wife.

But I saw what Tom didn't. I saw what seeing them together did to her, the way she straightened her spine and lifted her chin even as the light in her eyes retreated. I recognized her determination to keep a strong façade as everything beneath her crumbled.

She pulls back a few inches, opens her eyes, and looks up at me, confusion all over her face. I stroke my thumb along her jaw and smile for my audience. "You look tired. Let me get you to bed."

She cuts her eyes to Tom then back to me. "I want to wait and talk to Courtney."

I shake my head. "It's going to be a while. Come on. Let's get a shower and a nap." I tuck her hair behind her ear. "We'll come back later to talk to your friend."

Confusion still swims in her eyes, but she nods and takes my hand. "I should find Officer Gormong and make sure it's okay that I go."

"It's already taken care of." I nod to Tom and his wife and lead Janelle out of the room.

"Nice to, uh, meet you," Tom's wife says to my back, and I lift a hand in acknowledgment, not bothering to turn around.

Janelle is silent as we leave the station. Sunrise has tinted the horizon in amber, and the clatter of the city is muted in the early hour. I direct Janelle to the black

Lincoln SUV waiting for us in front.

"The Beverly Wilshire," I tell the driver after we climb in. That earns me a raised brow from Janelle, but she says nothing, only buckles in and stares out her window.

She doesn't break her silence until we're on the road and the driver is contending with the morning traffic. "How did you . . .?" She pulls her eyes from the window and looks at me, her eyes full of questions.

"Gormong called me last night. I used to work at that precinct," I say, as if that really explains my one-eighty from yesterday morning. "We'll talk later."

She skims her lips with two fingers, then stops herself. Her gaze shifts to the driver then back to me. "Okay. Later."

We ride in silence, and I try to focus on our next steps. I only have plans through tonight, and I need to figure out the best way to keep her safe after that. But no matter how hard I try to concentrate, I can't stop picturing her face when Tom pulled Bella into his arms, can't stop hearing her words to him before Bella arrived. *"Stop fucking with my heart."*

The broken parts of me recognize the broken parts of her, and it's so tempting to imagine our ragged edges fitting together, making us each whole where we haven't been for years.

That's not why I'm here. I didn't come to fix her broken heart or make her believe in love again. Fuck that. Maybe I have a weakness for her eyes, for the way she tastes. Maybe I'm haunted by the way she moaned when my mouth was between her legs. But I've learned from my mistakes. I don't trust her. I'm only here because the only way I know she's safe is if I'm holding her close. Despite her flaws, her safety is more important than my pride. I won't be able to live with myself if she gets hurt and I could have prevented it. Maybe keeping *this* woman safe will allow me to forgive myself for the one I failed.

When we get to the hotel, I instruct the driver to drop us at the service entrance at the back. I've arranged for a bellman to meet us here. Though I don't care if they take pictures of us together at this point, I don't need the press leaking her location. I'll need to set up a complete security detail before I'll risk this creep knowing her whereabouts. Even then, I'd rather keep it secret.

"Mr. Watts, I'll lead you to your room," the bellman says as we file in the back. He takes us up a service elevator and down a back hallway to our room. "There should be plenty of privacy here," he says as he opens the door for us and hands me a pair of key cards. "Please let us know if we can be of service."

I slip him a couple of fifties. He leaves as Janelle spins a slow circle to take in the room. She looks a little awestruck, which would be understandable for most people, but Janelle Crane comes from Hollywood royalty. She *is* Hollywood royalty. The Beverly Wilshire is her Holiday Inn.

I drop my bag in the closet and tug my shirt over my head. I need a shower and a few hours of sleep.

"We're sharing a room?" she asks, her eyes on my bare chest.

I take a deep breath and do my best to remind my body that I'm not here for fun, that this relationship is nothing but a ruse. But there's nothing fake about the way she looks at me. The chemistry between us is real. "That's the plan," I say, stepping forward. I can't help myself. When she's in the room, I need to be closer.

"Were you going to let me in on this *plan* at any point?"

I grunt. "Yeah, that must suck, having someone plan something that involves you and never let you in on it."

She folds her arms and her face hardens. "I don't have any patience for your tender ego right now. I've had a fucking shitty day. You need to start talking or I'm walking out that door. I don't care what kind of favors you called in to make sure no one saw us together."

"*There's* the spoiled princess," I mutter.

"What did you just call me?"

"I'm just pointing out that you're awfully demanding for a woman who owes me a little gratitude."

"Gratitude?" She shakes her head, obviously trying to make sense of my motivations.

I sympathize. I can't even process how I quickly I picked up and flew across the country for a woman I barely know—a woman who I wanted nothing to do with twenty-four hours ago. Any analysis makes me seriously question my own judgment, so I've chosen not to think about it at all.

"What do you want me to thank you for, exactly?" she asks. "For *kissing* me?"

"Sure." I take another step closer, and she has to crane her neck to look up at me. "Start there." My gaze drops to her lips. Goddamn, but I want to touch her again. And not for an audience this time. Just for me. For us.

"You want me to thank you," she says slowly, emphasizing each word, "for. Kissing. Me?"

My lips twitch. "Isn't it proper to thank a person for giving you something you enjoy, *princess*?"

"Fuck you."

I shrug. "That wasn't in my plans, but it could be arranged."

Her nostrils flare, and she presses a hand to my chest. If she intended to push me away, something stops her. Instead, she just rests it there as her gaze dips to my mouth and her lips part. "You're an asshole."

"Sorry, was that not in the script? Next time, tell me how your fake boyfriend is supposed to act. I'll try to do better." I squeeze my eyes shut. I'm being a dick, all because I don't trust myself around her.

"You have one hell of a chip on your shoulder," she says, and when I open my eyes, she's leaning closer. "Can't say that I blame you for that."

I could kiss her now. I could lead her to the bed and put my hand between her legs, seduce her with soft touches until we both forget what we're here hiding from. Maybe she'd let me fuck her, and I'd find out if her moan is as deep and throaty when I'm inside her as it is when my mouth is between her legs. The sex would be hard—fast and greedy and so fucking good.

Maybe it'd be better to get it out of our systems.

Maybe it's inevitable.

I'm calculating the best way to get her to the bed when she lifts her chin and whispers, "Thank you. Thank you for kissing me like that in front of Tom." The words are full of sincerity and vulnerability. They're a sucker punch to the gut.

"You're welcome." I draw in a deep breath, trying to remember all the reasons I shouldn't touch her. There were reasons. I'm almost sure of it. "I should get in the shower."

She steps back and lifts her shirt a few inches. The movement is hardly brazen, but it exposes her navel and the jewel pierced into it. The jewel I sucked into my mouth only two days ago. *Christ.*

"You want company?" she asks.

My gut knots and my cock is rock hard in an instant. Fuck yes, I want company, and not just any company. I very specifically want the company of the woman offering it. I want her naked and wet against the marble tile, squeezing me tight as I make her come under the spray. And while I do it, I want her eyes to look like they do right now. Vulnerable. Open. Trusting.

I swallow hard and nod to the bed. "You need some sleep. You should nap. We'll talk later." I turn and close the door before I can change my mind.

If I'm going to protect her, I have to think of her as the Hollywood princess who's cold and manipulative to her core. Because a vulnerable Janelle melts the ice I've carefully erected around my heart.

I strip the rest of my clothes and turn the shower as cold as it will go.

CHAPTER SIX

Janelle

WHEN THE BATHROOM DOOR CLICKS CLOSED behind Cade, I mime hari-kari then collapse onto the bed and stare at the ceiling.

Well, fuck.

I don't even know how I feel. There are way too many emotions swimming through my head for me to keep up. I'm turned on, pissed off, scared, confused, and exhausted. Okay, so exhaustion isn't technically an emotion, but when mental, physical, and emotional exhaustion peak together like this, fatigue becomes a force all of its own.

How can I feel so tired and so alive all at once?

Cade's eyes were on my lips, his mouth so close to mine. I was sure he was going to kiss me again. More than kiss me. I thought he might devour me. And what I wouldn't give to be devoured right now. To surrender myself to his touch, his mouth, his scent, until the terrifying previous day was washed away by the pleasure he's proven his hands can bring. One second, I thought I'd get my wish, and the next he was responding to my offer to join him in the shower by telling me to take a nap.

I squeeze my eyes shut and knock my head against the mattress in frustration. Why does he have to be so sexy? Why does he have to be so bitter and broody? Why did Cara have to break his heart and make him hate all actresses?

I shoot up to sit on the edge of the mattress and glare at the bathroom door. "And why is he even *here*?" I mumble.

The sound of water hitting tile softens, and I imagine him stepping under the spray, water sliding over all that hard muscle and bare skin.

I am so pathetic that if there were a village of pathetic people, they would honor me as their queen. I just invited myself to shower with a guy who has made it very clear that he detests everything I stand for. I just *offered myself* to a guy who is so fucking old school that he swooped into town unannounced, kissed me in front of my ex, and brought me to this hotel without any explanation. Seriously, to act any more like a caveman, he'd have to start dragging me around by my hair.

Not that I wasn't grateful for his impeccable timing at the station, but the asshole didn't even offer me the first shower.

I shudder. I've been in these clothes for a flight across the country and a night in the police station. I don't think I can stand them touching me for another minute, unless it's to throw them into a fire. But since

Mr. Caveman didn't think about stopping to get me clothes, it's not like I have anything to change into.

I open the closet and find one of those big, fluffy robes. *Sold.* I strip out of my dirty clothes and slide into it. My skin practically sings at the touch of the clean, soft fabric. After my shower, I'll call the front desk and ask them to do a little shopping for me.

My phone rings, and I fish it out of my purse. It's my agent.

"This day keeps getting better," I mutter, before swiping the screen to accept the call. "Merriellen!" I chirp in greeting.

"Janelle, how are you, dear?"

"I'm okay," I lie. Courtney's disappearance made the news, but Officer Gormong made it very clear that they don't want the surrounding details of the case leaked to the press yet. That includes the letters and the break-in at my condo. He requested that we only talk about it to trusted friends and family. My big-mouthed agent doesn't really fit the bill. "How are you, Merriellen?"

"Fabulous. Helen has agreed to meet me later this week and discuss what's best for the film. I think this is a very good sign. I saw the pictures of you and your cutie-pie boyfriend. Any chance I could tell her that'd you'd be open to bringing your beau to LA for dinner with her sometime?"

The mention of my would-be director has me shooting another glare at the bathroom door. This is the part where it would be very convenient to know exactly why Cade is here and why he's changed his mind about pretending to be my boyfriend—though I don't remember ever asking him to do any such thing—and to what extent he's willing to do said pretending.

"Janelle?" Merriellen says. "What do you think?"

I would never choose Cade to be my pretend boyfriend. My lover? Yes, please. But part of an ongoing charade that could make or break my career? There's a good chance we'd kill each other before a week was up. I'm not even sure I want to share this hotel room with him and his tangled web of mixed signals. "I'll see what I can arrange."

Really, what else can I say? It's not like I'm making actual plans. This is the equivalent of telling someone you'd love to catch up over drinks "someday." Everyone knows "someday" is elusive. When someday finally rolls around, my PR crisis will have passed and Cade can conveniently not be in my life anymore.

"Fantastic," Merriellen says. "Now tell me all the details. Is your detective as good in bed as Cara Fray says?"

* * *

Cade

Janelle isn't sleeping when I get out of the shower. She's put on one of the hotel's big terry cloth robes and curled into the chair by the window.

I'm not sure if this is better or worse than finding her

in bed.

I stood under the ice-cold spray of the shower and imagined her long legs tangling in the sheets, her hair spread out across the pillow. When my imagination drifted to her hand sliding between her legs, I not-so-easily redirected my thoughts to getting her back to New Hope. The sight of her now, however, slingshots my brain right back to the tangled sheets image. Only this time, I'm not imagining her alone.

I don't realize she's on the phone until I hear her speak.

"I'm safe," she says. "Yes . . . no. Don't worry about me. I'm fine. In fact," she says, giggling, "I'm in a beautiful room at the Beverly Wilshire."

Something surges in my chest, and I tell myself the unwelcome feeling is nothing more than aggravation over her disclosing her location. It's not jealousy that some other man might be treated to that bright, happy laughter. Who's she talking to? Did she call Tom as soon as I climbed in the shower? I can't make out the words, but I can make out the rumble of a deep voice coming from the phone.

"No, I'm not alone." She's silent for a beat, then says, "Cade's with me," and I feel a rush of satisfaction. Whoever she's talking to, I like the idea of him knowing I'm here.

She traces a pattern on the chair's upholstery for long seconds as she listens, still seemingly oblivious to my presence. "I promise I'll explain when I'm back in town. It's complicated . . . Yeah, well, Hanna is overprotective. It's not like you were the perfect prince when you two started dating."

Hanna. Which means she's talking to her brother. Relief loosens whatever unreasonable emotions were holding my lungs in a vise. My heavy exhale gets Janelle's attention, and she holds up a single finger to indicate she's almost done.

She grins at the phone then laughs. "I agree. What? *You* said it first. I'm just agreeing she could have done better." She laughs again, so much more relaxed than she was fifteen minutes ago. "Okay. Give my nieces kisses for me. Love you too." She ends the call and turns. "Nice shower?"

"Sure." I sink into the chair across from her and instantly regret it. From this position, I can see her bare thighs peeking out from the slit in the robe. I scan the room and find her clothes in a neat pile on the dresser. She's naked under all that fluffy white cotton. The smooth skin at the curve of her calf makes my hands itch to part the robe farther. Higher. To follow the path north to other stretches of softness I haven't gotten to explore nearly long enough.

I force my gaze in the opposite direction that my hands want to go. Her toenails are painted light pink, and her feet have the prettiest arch to them.

Since when do I care about feet?

God help me.

"Sorry I, um"—she clears her throat— "invited myself to your shower."

My head snaps up. We're going to talk about this? For real? Most women I know would have never mentioned it again. "Not a problem."

She steadies her gaze on me, studying my face as if she's trying to figure me out. "You kissed me. It was a very *convincing* kiss."

"Tom was standing there. He needed to see that." I draw in a ragged breath. "There will be more of that in the coming days—kissing in front of people just so they see us. It would be a mistake to confuse what we need to do for an audience for what we do in private."

She's silent for a beat, as if she's turning that over in her mind. "You may have missed your calling as an actor."

I give her a hard look. I didn't say anything about acting. Kissing her is easy. It's the *not* kissing that's going to be the death of me.

Her gaze slides over me, from my bare feet to my jeans and tank, halting at my face. "Are you feeling all right? Your lips are a little blue."

"Cold shower." Setting my jaw, I shrug as if it's every day I have to freeze my balls off to resist a woman.

The corners of her mouth twitch, but she doesn't comment. "What is this?" she asks, waving her hand between us. "You're here and suddenly going to act like my boyfriend? Why?"

"Isn't that what you want? Isn't that the solution to all your problems?"

She shifts in her chair, folding her legs under her, and the robe gapes above her breasts. There's nothing indecent about the amount of skin she's showing, but try telling that to my sex-starved brain. "You made it very clear you wanted nothing to do with my efforts to fix my reputation," she says. "What changed?"

Right. The explanation I was too much of a dick to give her before my arctic shower. "Officer Gormong is an old friend. He called me because he thought you and I were together. His wife had seen the pictures."

"I haven't had a chance to set the story straight." She rubs a hand over her face. "I got home and saw the flowers on my bed, and then everything got a little crazy."

"He thought I'd want to know what happened to you," I continue. "When he told me, I didn't correct his assumptions about our relationship. I decided it would be better not to."

"I never intended to get you involved. There was another guy at the party Matt had hired to . . ." She shifts awkwardly. "Matt hired a guy to play the part of my boyfriend. I knew he'd be there dressed as Batman. We were going to introduce him to my family and friends and make out at the party. Then we were going to pretend to get engaged and pray my director would take note and forgive my lapse of judgment with Tom."

As much as I'd like to think she's as conniving as Cara, I've thought a lot in the last day about the look on her face when she lifted up my mask. She was surprised, and then she ran in the other direction. *I* was the one who chased after her. "You kissed the wrong Batman," I say.

Part of me wishes I gave her the chance to explain as much back at Nate's house, but it wouldn't have changed anything. She's still part of a world I can't stomach. My attraction to her and any illusions said attraction is planting in my brain have nothing to do with my decision to come here.

She takes a deep breath. "When I took you to Maggie and Asher's, I had no intention of involving you in my plans to repair my reputation."

I lean forward, my elbows on my knees, and study her. "But by the time you took me to Asher's, you'd seen my face. You knew I wasn't your hired stud." It's not a question, and she doesn't reply. "Why'd you do it? Why'd you leave that party with me when the guy you needed for your plan was waiting inside?"

Her cheeks flare pink, and she cuts her eyes to the side. "I guess I was running."

"From what?"

"From the plan Matt had already set in motion." She shrugs but holds my gaze. "I don't care for what Matt Hailey does, and I think what he did to you was unconscionable."

"What do you know about it?"

"Not much. Enough. I've proven that I'm not above using Matt's services," she says, grimacing, "but I would *never* lie to someone the way Cara lied to you."

"And yet you were willing to lie to your friends and family. To tell them a relationship was real when it wasn't."

"Touché." She gives a sad smile. "I'm sorry about the way it unfolded, and I'm sorry I haven't had a chance to untangle you from my lies."

"I'm not."

Her lips part in surprise. "What?"

"I'm not sorry. It's true I didn't want to have

anything to do with the plans you made with Matt, but now I'm glad I have an excuse to stay close to you."

"Is this about Cara?" she asks. "Are you trying to get back at her or something?"

It is about Cara, but not in the way she thinks. "I don't give a shit what Cara thinks about me and my love life. Not anymore."

"So . . ." She arches a brow. "Am I understanding you? You're actually offering to pretend to be my boyfriend so I can fix my reputation?"

"I'm pretending to be your boyfriend so I have an excuse to stay close to you and keep you *safe* until they catch this guy. I'm not doing interviews or going out of my way to make the media think we're madly in love, but I'll be by your side. If you can resist your ex's bullshit and not fuck around with him, I imagine you'll get what you set out for."

Her eyes narrow. "I'm not having an affair with Tom."

I shrug. "Not my business."

"I know the press makes it sound like he and I have been sleeping together, but I wouldn't do that. It really was just that one night and just that one kiss. He said he'd left her. A lie, and that's on him. But he also said he missed me. He said leaving me was the biggest mistake he'd ever made. I believed him, and that's on me."

There it is. That goddamned vulnerability. I weave around it like I'm dodging a punch. "Your past doesn't matter to me beyond what I need to know to protect you."

She rolls her eyes. "Not that I don't appreciate your Rambo efforts to save the day, but doesn't this seem like an overreaction? Someone has been sending me creepy letters and then broke into my apartment and left me a creepy message. Courtney's temporary disappearance may not even be connected, and she's *fine*. I'm not sure the situation calls for you to play bodyguard."

"They found Courtney at her house."

"I know." She frowns. "And she wasn't hurt, right?"

"She doesn't remember anything from the time she was missing. She was partying at an LA club and the next thing she remembers, she was waking up in the bathroom at Highland Park Station. They're doing blood work right now, and I expect it will show high doses of Rohypnol or a similar drug. That would explain why she doesn't remember, and why she can't explain the ligature marks on her wrists and ankles."

"Ligature marks?" she repeats in a whisper. "Like someone had her tied up."

"They're also performing a full physical exam. And a rape kit." I pause and allow that to sink in before I continue. "This isn't *nothing,* Janelle. This is real and it's scary, and until they arrest whoever's behind it, you're in danger."

She shivers and wraps her arms around herself. "Who is he?"

"We don't know. Honestly, at this point we don't have any evidence that the perp is male." We don't know much of anything, and considering how careful the perp has been thus far, I don't expect Courtney would have been left in that bathroom with any kind of DNA evidence on her. "I know you didn't ask me to come here or to stay with you, but I need to. And I need you to promise me you'll take this seriously."

"Of course." She stands, looking a little dazed, and I feel like a dick for the second time since we walked into this room. I hate seeing her scared, but fuck, she *needs* to be scared. "I need a shower and some sleep."

"I need a few hours myself," I say, eyeing her cautiously. "I'll take the couch."

"No, please. Take the bed. I can sleep anywhere."

"I'll take the couch," I repeat, going to the closet for extra pillows and blankets.

I'm settling onto my makeshift bed when I hear the shower turn on. I force my eyes to close, wondering if it's even possible to doze off with so much lust and adrenaline poisoning my blood. The worry hardly has a chance to settle before I fall asleep.

When I wake up, the sun is low in the sky, and the room is quiet. I stand and stretch quietly. I hope Janelle was able to sleep too, but I don't want to wake her.

Only, when I turn to the bed, she's not there. "Janelle?" I call, spinning slowly and already knowing I'm alone in the room.

Tamping down instinctive panic, I search the room, check the bathroom, step into the hallway, and even look in the fucking closet.

"Janelle!" I call again, louder this time.

She's gone.

CHAPTER SEVEN

Janelle

"I SHOULD REALLY GO," I say over the music for the third time, but there's no conviction to my voice. I don't want to go anywhere right now—not because hanging with Matthew is so great, but because every alternative I've come up with blows.

Matt shrugs and signals the waitress for another round. "Or you could keep me company."

"Hmm . . ." I pretend to think it over. "Sure. I guess."

Really, there's nothing to think about. I could stay here at the HiLo, sipping cosmos and escaping reality for another thirty minutes, or I could return to that too-small hotel room with broody Cade of the broad shoulders and smoldering eyes. Cade, whose words and actions seem to contradict each other in every moment. He doesn't like me, but he flew across the country to protect me. He doesn't think we should touch in private, but he looks at me like he wants to lick every inch of me.

Maybe I'm projecting on that last one. It could be that I think he wants to lick every inch of me because I want him to. Or because I want to lick every inch of *him.*

The waitress brings my martini and I sip, absently tugging at the too-short skirt Matt bought for me when I asked him to bring me clothes. On one side of me, Jamaal sits, quietly scanning the crowd and generally looking like a badass. He's wearing a black suit and his shoulders take up half the booth. Jamaal worked personal security for my brother for years, and I still consider him a good friend. When Matt texted about meeting tonight, I knew I shouldn't leave the hotel without some sort of bodyguard. I'm still pretty freaked about what may have happened to Courtney while she was missing, and I figured Cade wouldn't be quite so pissed about me slipping out if he knew I had extra protection.

On the other side of me, Matt prattles on about some diva who just landed her first big film role. "She thought I'd work for her for free," Matt says. "For, like, the honor, or the experience or some shit."

I pretend to listen to Matt's gossip, but my mind is on Cade. Any number of people are capable of keeping me safe until the police track down this creep. Why is Cade so determined to do the job himself? He's so hellbent on protecting me that he's willing to fake a relationship, something he sneered at just yesterday morning? It doesn't add up. There's more he's not telling me.

Pathetically, I keep circling back to our conversation when we first arrived at the hotel.

"Fuck you."

"That wasn't in my plans, but it could be arranged."

If only. If Cade were really interested in fucking me, I wouldn't be here right now. I'd be exploring the muscles that contour his chest and abs. Finding out what noises he makes when he comes. It's not fair, really. During our one night together, he explored my body with his hands and mouth, but I never got my turn.

He's not like the guys here in LA—the kind who wax their chests to make their muscles more prominent. Cade doesn't need to wax and would probably laugh at anyone who suggested it. He is one hundred percent male, with a smattering of chest hair to prove it. I'd like to trace my fingers along the path of soft hair beneath his navel, like to wake him from a deep sleep by following it with my tongue.

"What the fuck do you think you're doing?"

I snap my head up. As if my fantasies alone conjured him, Cade is standing at the end of our table, glaring at me. It could be the martinis talking, but he looks absolutely edible—jeans slung low on his hips and a dark button-up shirt rolled up his forearms. This morning's stubble has gotten thicker, making him look a little wild. Dangerous. Even his scowl is sexy, and I want to rub against him and purr.

Jamaal is halfway to his feet when I grab his wrist to stop him. "It's okay. That's Cade," I say. Jamaal settles back into our booth, not relaxed but at least not ready to pounce.

Matt winces, hunching his shoulders as if Cade might take a swing at him. "Watts. Good to see you again." Matt offers his hand.

Cade ignores Matt and shifts that hot and angry gaze back to me. He opens his mouth to speak, then seems to reconsider as he closes it. Irritation washes over his features as he asks, "Are you okay?" He's practically shouting to be heard over the music.

I lift my martini and take a long drink, nearly draining it. "I'm grrrrrreat!" I say it like the tiger on that cereal commercial, but Cade does not seem amused.

"Are you—" I'm guessing the end of that sentence was going to be something along the lines of *fucking kidding me*? or *trying to drive me insane?* but he snaps his mouth shut again. He gives a dark look to each of my male companions before releasing a breath. "I need to make a call. Don't. Move." He looks at a guy standing a few feet behind him and points to our table before pulling out his phone and disappearing around the corner.

"That must be our babysitter," I say, studying the tall man who's watching us with folded arms. "My babysitter hired a babysitter. You think that means he's come to his senses and now he's going to ditch me?"

"I don't think he trusts you enough to ditch you." Jamaal gives me a look. "Looks like the *princess* is in trouble."

I'm sorry I told them about Cade calling me *princess*. But *damn,* it annoys me when he does it. "He's definitely angry," I mutter. "What's new?"

Matt grins. "Girl, he's not just angry. There's so much sexual tension between you two, it's like he . . ." He rubs his hands together, trying to think of the words.

"Like he wants to spank your ass," Jamaal fills in, and I giggle. I can imagine that, strangely. I've never been spanked before—sexually or otherwise—but I can *absolutely* imagine Cade pulling me onto his lap, pulling up my skirt, and smacking my ass with his open hand. Something buzzes up my spine at the thought and then spirals low and hot in my belly. I don't actually *like* the idea, do I? This man seriously screws with my brain.

"He may have been in love with Cara," Matt says, "but he *never* looked at *her* like that. Damn. Please let me get you two in front of a camera. If you could talk him into just one interview . . ."

I glare at him. We've been over this. "Did that look like a man who could be talked into anything?"

Cade reappears at the end of the table, meets my gaze, and lifts his chin. "Let's go."

As in, go back to that hotel room and have Cade glare at me like I'm the worst thing that ever happened to him? "I'm not going anywhere," I say. I don't care that I sound childish. Life kind of sucks right now, and I think I'm entitled to a little childish behavior. "I'm having a good time, and I'm not ready to leave."

"Do you *want* me to throw you over my shoulder and drag you out of here?" Cade asks.

Folding my arms, I return his glare. "Is that what a loving boyfriend would do?"

Jamaal wipes the humor from his face and leans

90

forward enough to send the message that he's with me, and I won't be going anywhere I don't want to. Jamaal is as mean-spirited as a kitten, but no one knows that by looking at him. He gives intimidating glares like it's his job. And since my brother still has him on retainer, tonight, it is.

Unfortunately, Cade is unfazed. "Test me, princess."

Jamaal's badass expression falters. He snickers and says under his breath, "Gonna spank your ass."

Matt slides out of our corner booth and motions to the spot next to me. "Come on, man. Join us!"

Cade sneers at him. Then he turns to me. "You want to stay?"

"Yes!" I drain my martini and hold the empty glass to the passing waitress. "Another round, please! And a beer for my *boyfriend* this time, too."

"Fine," Cade says, grabbing my extended hand. A trickle of foreboding creeps down my spine as he sets the glass on the table and pulls me from the booth. "Then let's dance."

He drags me to the dance floor, moving so fast I practically trip over my own feet trying to keep up with him. When I open my mouth to complain, he pulls me into his arms.

I didn't sleep after my shower. I was too busy making arrangements for tonight and trying not to stare at how gorgeous Cade was when he slept. I caught a brief nap on the way here, but days of sleep deprivation are catching up to me. I want to melt into Cade and have his big hands stroke my back. I want him to be the boyfriend he's pretending to be and make me believe everything is okay.

But he isn't my boyfriend, and he doesn't relax at the contact of our bodies. Not at all. He's one solid block of tension. I've spent most of the night second-guessing my decision to let him do me a favor he doesn't owe me. The resentment rolling off him in waves is only feeding my doubts.

"Why are you so *angry* with me?" I link my hands behind his neck. "You're *always* so angry with me."

"Are you fucking kidding me?"

Rising onto my toes, I position my mouth by his ear. "No one's going to believe you're my boyfriend if you hold me like you're afraid you might catch something."

One second we're standing there, barely moving on the dance floor. The next, he's spinning me around, and I'm trapped between his body and the wall. He has one hand at my neck, the other at my waist, one thick thigh between my legs.

"You wanna know why I'm *angry*?" He presses closer. My already-short skirt hikes higher up my hips, and I'm treated to the delicious pressure of his thigh pressing into the lace of my panties. "Maybe because you're reckless. Selfish. Immature. Maybe because for the last three hours you've been boozing it up with your buddies while I was picturing you bound and helpless to some obsessive maniac."

Before I can reply, his mouth is on mine. This isn't like the seductive kisses we shared on our first night together, and it lacks the tenderness of the kiss he gave me at the station. This kiss matches his mood. It's hot and angry. Demanding and possessive. This is the kiss of a man who very well could throw his woman over his shoulder and drag her home. The kiss of a man whose woman would relish such treatment.

I shouldn't be that woman. I shouldn't even *pretend* to be her. But *should* has nothing to do with the way I open my mouth and slip my tongue inside to taste him. *Should* has nothing to do with me shifting my stance, lifting one knee to give his thigh better access to my aching center. When Cade touches me, *should* goes out the window and is replaced by *must.*

I *must* pull him closer. I *must* learn how his neck tastes. I *must* dissolve into his kiss until the world disappears. Then even *must* falls away and I am nothing but this ache where need becomes pleasure and pleasure becomes need. He called me reckless, and right now I am. With him, that's what I become.

When he tears his mouth from mine, I gasp at the loss.

"Is that better?" he asks, rubbing his face against my neck and marking me with his stubble. "If I hold you like this." The hand at my waist slides down until he's cupping my ass. "Touch you like this." The hand on my neck dips to skim the tops of my breasts. "Would that be enough?" He opens his mouth against my neck and sucks. Hard. "What's it going to take to get you to listen to me?"

"Cade . . ." Maybe that last martini was a mistake, or maybe his mouth and hands on me are just too much, because I don't understand what he's talking about. I knew Cade wouldn't be happy about me leaving without him, and I knew even with Jamaal by my side, my decision to spend time in public would make him uncomfortable. To be fair, that was why I left the note instead of waking him. I knew he wouldn't approve.

The flash of a camera tears me from my lust-induced trance and reminds me we're not alone.

"Janelle!" a man calls behind me. "Is this your new boyfriend?"

Jamaal is there before I can blink, stepping forward to block me and Cade from the photographer.

"How does it feel to know your girlfriend is fucking around with her ex-husband?" the photographer shouts from behind Jamaal, and the question makes my blood chill. I don't want to be here anymore.

"I'll leave with you now," I tell Cade.

He doesn't miss a beat. He leads the way to the door as I mouth *thank you* to Jamaal. I catch Matthew's eye on the way out, and he looks way too pleased with himself.

Somehow I'm not surprised to see Cade has a car waiting, and yet the press of the crowd and the flashes of more cameras startle me.

Fucking Matt. No doubt I have him to thank for this.

The babysitter from earlier opens the door, and Cade wraps his arm around my shoulders as I lower my head and climb in. Cade takes the seat beside mine then takes my wrist and tugs me toward him until I practically tumble sideways into his lap.

"Come here," he says, his voice gruff as he leads me to straddle him.

I obey. Instinct overtaking reason, I position a knee on either side of his hips and loop my arms behind his neck. My skirt hikes up my thighs and the hard length of him presses against me through his jeans. And thank God, because I don't care about anything but getting my body as close to his as possible as quickly as possible.

"Cameras," he murmurs softly as he reaches to power down the windows. As they open, his hands are in my hair and he's crushing his mouth to mine.

If it weren't for that word, that reminder that this is just pretend for him, I'd probably be grinding against him right about now. I'd be kissing him with all the need I feel every time I've set eyes on him since the party. Instead, I hold back. I sweep my tongue across his lips and angle my head for the cameras outside the car, but I don't throw myself into it. I don't allow myself to fantasize that this is more to him than a role he's determined to play.

When the car slides smoothly into traffic, I break the kiss and press the button to roll up the tinted windows. "Thanks," I mutter, forcing a smile. "You definitely played the part of Janelle Crane's boyfriend like a pro tonight." I start to climb off his lap, but he puts a hand on each thigh and stills me.

"If you think you can just put yourself in danger and go *clubbing* anytime you like, there's no point in me acting like your boyfriend," he growls in my ear. "If you're going to leave without giving me the slightest clue where you've disappeared to, we might as well forget all of this."

I pull back so I can see his face. His gaze dips to my lips, and his eyes are clouded with lust. "I wasn't in any danger in there," I say, and his jaw goes tight with anger.

Tonight, Cade's different somehow. As if his anger has cracked open his hard exterior, exposing a hint of the vulnerability he hides behind it.

"Fuck, Janelle, did you hear nothing I told you earlier? This guy is—"

"That's why I called Jamaal. He's a professional bodyguard, *and* a trusted family friend. He worked for my brother for years."

He mutters a curse, and his grip tightens on my thighs. He flips a switch on the door and a divider slowly rises from the seats in front of us, giving us privacy from our driver. "Do you know who I was calling when I first found you? The police. I had to call Gormong to tell him you *weren't* actually missing."

"Why would you tell the police that I'm missing?"

"It's not just that you made me look like a fucking fool," Cade says, going on as if I didn't speak. It's as if now that he's started touching me, he can't stop. One hand releases its hold on my thigh and settles at the small of my back. His thumb slides under my shirt and across the skin just above my waistband. "It's not just that I've spent the last three hours worried sick looking for you." The anger rides low in his voice, a wicked undercurrent I'd be wise to remember lurks beneath his lust.

"You've been looking for me for three hours?" It's a struggle to focus on our conversation when every brain cell wants to examine the way he's touching me. The rough pad of his thumbs against the skin; how the slow, rhythmic sweeps across my spine feel like the most intimate touch we've shared.

I shake my head to clear the fog. "It took you three hours to check the place I named in my note?"

"I thought I'd check here, even though I was sure you weren't idiotic enough to— What note?"

I smile. This guy is unreal. I can see it beneath the anger. The honest-to-God *worry*. The kind that eats you from the inside, frazzles your brain, and makes you literally ill. The kind of worry that makes a man run all over LA looking for someone. I rest my head against his chest. "I left you a note on the end table, by the remote control. Matt wanted to meet. I thought I should bring him up to speed on where we stood. I thought it'd be better to do it without you, given your history."

"And why the fuck did you turn off your phone?"

Fumbling, I pull my phone from my back pocket and press the power button. Frowning, I turn the black screen to Cade. "I guess it died." The martinis are probably to blame. I don't know the last time I went three hours without looking at my phone. Unless we're counting the night of Halloween when I was naked and Cade had his mouth on me.

He swallows hard. "You left me a note."

"You thought I just took off while you were sleeping and didn't tell you where to find me?"

"I— You're *sure?*"

"I'm sure. I'm sorry you didn't see it." I can't help it. I have to touch him. I drop my phone in the seat beside us and lift my hand to run it along the edge of his jaw. "I didn't mean to scare you."

"It was still a stupid decision. Matt could have met you in our room, or you could have talked on the phone."

I'm not going to spend the length of this investigation cloistered in some hotel room, but I decide not to charge into that discussion. Not now, when the tension is finally oozing out of him, slow but steady.

I graze my thumb over his bottom lip, dying to kiss him again. "Why do you even care what happens to me?"

"Because it's who I am. I protect people from bad guys."

"You can't protect everyone."

"But I can protect you." He holds my gaze, as if willing me to understand. "I need to take care of you."

My heart tumbles at those words, but I tell myself not to read too much into them. This is a man who needs to be the hero and protector. The worry I see in his eyes isn't about budding love or affection, even if I want it to be. He's offering a favor, not his heart. But I've never met anyone like him, and I want more. Maybe I'll regret it, but right now, I'll take as much of him as he'll give.

"Take care of me?" I give an experimental rotation of my hips, rubbing myself against him. "Promises, promises."

His fingers slip under my skirt until they skim the lace at my hip. With a long, jagged exhale, he squeezes his eyes shut even as he holds my body tight against his and the hard length of his shaft presses against my center. "You're killing me, you know that? Resisting you while keeping you close may just destroy me."

I slide my hand between our bodies and unbutton his jeans. He curses softly and I whisper, "Then stop resisting."

CHAPTER EIGHT

Cade

J ANELLE'S GIVING ME PERMISSION to do exactly what I want to do. *Stop resisting.*

When I found her at the club, every ounce of my fear combusted into anger. It was a relief. Anger keeps me sharp. Focused. On my game. I liked the anger and planned to use it like a shield. Then I got her on the dance floor and against that wall. With her mouth under mine, I fought to hold on to that focus, but the lust pumping through me threatened to wash it away.

Now I'm losing my control again.

I grab Janelle's wrist, stopping her before she lowers my zipper. I need to get a handle on my erratic emotions, on my . . . fuck, my *need* for her.

Her eyes snap up to my face, and she backs away but I hold her still before she can climb off my lap, my fingers curling into the soft skin of her thigh. "Stay."

She worries her bottom lip between her teeth. "You send some seriously mixed signals. Has anyone ever told you that?"

I tuck a lock of hair behind her ear. "No one's ever left me quite so conflicted as you do."

"What's the conflict? I want you." Her gaze drops to my hand on her thigh. "I think you want me."

Of course I do. Who wouldn't? She's so fucking beautiful. I skim my thumb over her bottom lip. "You've been drinking."

"I'm not drunk." She takes my thumb between her teeth and bites it gently. "Should I remind you that I hadn't had a drop of alcohol when I invited you to join me in the shower?"

I groan—at that reminder, and at the feel of her tongue wrapping around my thumb. Need coils in my gut and my cock aches with the ideas that tongue inspires, so I pull my hand away and fist it at my side. "I'm here to protect you." I'm reminding myself as much as her. "Sex will only complicate things. I don't know how long it will take to find this guy."

"Exactly," she whispers. "I'm not sure how long I can handle this push and pull between us." She repositions her hips over mine and shifts until our bodies are notched together.

After this day, after denying myself what she offered this morning and then being so terrified I'd lost her to some maniac tonight, my need for her is no longer a rational thing. I'm not sure it ever was.

"I'm not her," she says.

"What?"

"She fucked you, and I can see why you'd expect the same from me. I'm not Cara."

Bringing up Cara now feels like an oversimplification of our situation. At the same time, it feels like the only truth that matters. She's not Cara. It's true. It took Cara months to have a hold of my emotions in the way Janelle has managed to do in just days. "I know you're not."

She looks so vulnerable. I cup her face in my hands, and I kiss her. I can't get enough of kissing her. The way she seems to melt into me, the way she sweeps her tongue inside my mouth, the way she tastes—every touch makes me want the next while slowly chipping away at my common sense.

"God, you make me feel . . ." She bites her lip and looks away.

"Finish that sentence. What do I make you feel?"

She turns back to me. "Confused."

"I guess that goes both ways, then. You confuse the hell out of me. But that wasn't what you were going to say. What do I make you feel, sweetheart?"

"Impulsive. Achy." She licks her lips. They're pink and just a little swollen. I want to see what they look like after a night in my bed, after I've sucked and abused them. "A scary amount of wild."

That word reminds me of our first night together. I told her I wanted her to be wild. To fuck my face as I went down on her. "Tell me what else I make you feel."

"Brave. I've never been like this."

Taking my hand, she presses it to the side of her neck where her pulse dances under my fingertips. "My heart races every time you step close. My body aches just because you walk in the room." She pauses for a beat, then takes a breath. "Tell me it's a little like that for you."

I see the truth in her eyes. She needs my reassurance right now. She needs to know she's wanted. She should know. She's a fucking actress, adored the world around, but she needs me to tell her, and even if it's foolish I can't deny her that.

"It's not a little like that," I whisper. Just as she starts to pull away, I explain. "It's worse. I want you so much, it's killing me. I wanted you in the shower with me this morning. I wanted to spread you out on that big bed, wanted to find out if you tasted as sweet as I remembered." My hand grazes the side of her neck and dips down to the soft swell of her breasts. "You want to know what I imagined doing to you? How often I think about tasting you again?"

"Show me."

I grab a fistful of her shirt, not bothering to be gentle as I yank it down. She's not wearing a bra beneath the low-cut top, and I lower my mouth to her exposed breast. I circle her nipple with my tongue and then suck until she moans. I've been hard since I kissed her on the dance floor, since the moment lust and want were so potent in my blood they overrode my anger and made every intention I had go blurry. The sound of her moan only intensifies the ache in my dick. "You make me crazy. I can't decide if I should stay far away from you or keep you as close as possible."

She reaches behind her neck and her shirt falls, pooling around her waist and exposing her breasts to my hands and mouth.

"You're perfect." I cup a breast in each hand and graze her nipples with my thumbs. "I could look at you for hours. But I'd rather touch you. Feel you. Listen to the sounds you make when you come."

"Let me." She strokes me through my jeans, gently at first, and then with more pressure. "I want you in my hand." Sliding to the floorboard, she positions herself on her knees. "And since I didn't get to do it in the shower . . . in my mouth."

Christ. She goes for my zipper, and all my restraint is gone. Not that I had much to begin with. I don't want any restraint, couldn't give two fucks that she could stomp on my heart at the end of this. I just want her. Her mouth. Her lips. Her tongue. All of her dirty promises.

Helping her, I push my pants and boxer briefs down my hips until my cock springs free. She wraps it in her fist. There are no teasing touches, just her firm grip, the pleasure that jackhammers up my spine, and the sound of her moan filling my ears.

She rubs me in long, even strokes, and then leans forward, a breath away from my tip, and looks up at me through her thick, dark lashes.

"Tell me you want this," she says, and I feel her ragged exhale against the sensitive head of my cock. "Tell me you want my mouth half as much as I want to put it on you."

I stroke my thumb over her cheek and take a fistful of her hair. "I want your mouth so much I might come the second your lips wrap around me."

She licks her lips. "Keep your hand in my hair. Tell

me if I should . . . change something I'm doing."

Again, I think I catch a glimpse of that vulnerability in her eyes, but before I can turn it over and examine it, she slides her mouth over me and my thoughts scatter. Her mouth is so hot and wet, and this is so much better than every one of my countless fantasies about it. I push my head back against the seat, but I don't close my eyes. I wouldn't miss a second of this sight. The way her mouth stretches around my cock, the flush of her skin as she works me over.

Part of my brain is aware of our surroundings—the traffic on the other side of the tinted windows, the driver in front of the privacy glass—but those facts fade with every stroke of her tongue. My reaction to her doesn't make any sense, but it's so primal I can't reason it away. Everything about Janelle turns me on.

She moans softly, and the vibration has my hips lifting off the seat, pushing my cock deeper before I can catch myself. I pull back, but her hands go to my hips, urging me forward and giving her a better angle to take me deep.

For the first time in my life, I'm grateful for the LA traffic. I don't want this to end. Not yet. I need to soak up every second of the heat of her mouth sliding over me. The sight of her bare breasts as she moves. I forget everything that kept me tangled in knots tonight and memorize the sight of her like this.

I don't know how much time has passed—seconds, minutes, hours—but when my orgasm bears down on me, it's too soon.

"Janelle," I say in a hoarse whisper. "Sweetheart,

I'm gonna come."

She moans in response and cups my balls in her hand. When I come, it's hard and fast, and she keeps me deep in her mouth so I can feel her squeeze my dick as she swallows.

Holy shit.

She pulls back slowly. I tuck myself back into my briefs and pull my jeans back up my hips, suddenly too aware of where we are and what she just did for me.

Avoiding my gaze, she repositions her top, hiding those perfect tits from me and securing the strap behind her neck.

When she climbs into the seat beside me, I growl, "Where do you think you're going?"

"My seat?"

"Your seat is in my lap." I have to touch her, to feel her body against mine and give her even a fraction of the pleasure she just gave me.

Obeying, she straddles me like she did earlier. Her cheeks are pink, as if she's embarrassed. She's such a contradiction—just sucked me off in the car but is embarrassed about climbing onto my lap.

"Better?" she asks.

"I'll be better when I finally have you safe in the room again." A lie. Being alone with her won't make me feel any better. I won't be better until I'm buried deep inside her. Maybe not even then. This woman does things to me. Like sends me into such a panic that I don't even look for a fucking note when she's missing, then gets me so hard that I let her suck me off in the back of a car. She has me breaking every rule I have about getting involved with actresses and Hollywood, and I don't even care.

"Aren't I safe right now? I'm with you, aren't I?"

I kiss her swollen mouth, slowly sucking her bottom lip between my teeth before pulling back. "I'm ashamed to admit that you distract the fuck out of me."

She smiles. "I think I like it when you're distracted. Hire someone else for security. Jamaal will watch for bad guys, and I'll distract you."

"I saw how close he was sitting to you." I saw it and didn't like it. Jealousy isn't an emotion I feel often, but they seemed so comfortable around each other. For a split second, I was consumed by how much *I* wanted that. "I'm not so sure Jamaal wasn't just as distracted by you as I am."

Giggling, she shakes her head. "No. Uh, I'm not his type."

"You're every man's type, princess," I say, but she stares at me and I realize what she means. "He doesn't like women?"

"Not romantically, no."

Good. "What did he say to you? Back at the table?" I take her hand in mine and lace our fingers together. "When I was trying to get you to leave, he dropped the badass routine for a minute. He laughed and whispered something to you."

She ducks her head and buries her face in my chest. "Nothing."

I take her chin in my hand and tilt her face up to mine.

"I promise he wasn't whispering sweet nothings,"

she says, biting back a smile.

"What *was* he whispering?"

"He said you looked like you wanted to spank me." Something flares in her eyes, and I swallow hard, because *damn.* "Do you?"

"I can honestly say that before tonight, spanking a woman has never appealed to me."

"And after tonight?"

"If I thought smacking your ass would help you make better decisions, I'd consider it." I study her for a beat. "You scared the shit out of me."

She sighs. "I'm sorry. I am. I knew you'd be unhappy about me going out, but frankly, Cade, I know you have this alpha caveman thing going on, but I'm not the kind of girl who wants some guy bossing her around. I'm a grown woman, and I am capable of taking care of myself."

"I imagine Courtney thought the same thing before she was drugged." I draw in a deep breath. I need this reminder as much as she does—all the reasons I need to keep my head on straight and not let lust shut down my brain. "I saw you in that club, drinking, laughing, dressed like *this*, and I imagined the creep who's after you sitting in there watching you. Waiting to make his move. These clothes show twice as much as they cover. More."

"Does that bother you? That I'm showing this much skin?" She wiggles in my lap as she asks, and her skirt inches up her thighs.

I slide my hands behind her and cup her ass in my hands. Fuck, but she's perfect. Every inch, every curve.

"Under normal circumstances, no." My gaze drops to her cleavage. "Despite what you think of me, I'm not some *caveman* who thinks he should have a say in how women dress. It's your body."

"*But*," she says, and I sigh.

"But tonight I'd rather you hadn't drawn so much attention to yourself."

"This is just how people dress for that club. *Not* dressing like this would draw attention to me."

"I'd still rather you hadn't gone there at all." I trace her jaw with my knuckle. "Jamaal might have your best interests at heart, but he can't follow you into the ladies' room."

I can tell she wants to argue but she's holding back. "Why did you think to check for me at the HiLo?"

She doesn't know. Jesus. "It's the last place Courtney remembers before her blackout. We're guessing that's where she was drugged."

Her breath catches. "I didn't know that."

"I was beginning to suspect as much."

"It was our favorite club," she says. "Back when we were doing *Roommates,* we spent a ton of time at the HiLo."

"Another reason to avoid the place. This guy—or woman, or whoever—is obsessed with everything that ties you to your role on *Roommates.*"

"I wouldn't have gone there if I'd known, but you can't expect me to stay cloistered until you find this guy. Be reasonable."

"Reasonable? I'd rather be *smart*, princess. For all we know, Matt could be the one sending the letters. He could be the one who broke into your condo. The one who drugged Courtney and abducted her. Maybe he lured you there tonight to drug your drink."

"Matt? You're kidding, right?"

"My point is, I don't want you out of my sight until we know who we can trust. It's temporary."

She shakes her head. "I appreciate you trying to protect me. I really do, but I'm not going to let some creep scare me into the shadows. I can't just hide. I need to live my life."

"You'll be safe. That's all that matters."

Turning her head, she looks at the traffic out the window. "I'll go out of my mind."

"Like I went out of my mind when I thought you were missing." I can't even think about those three hours without my gut knotting. The need to touch her surges. Even having her this close isn't enough to put all tonight's fears to rest.

"I don't know what I did to make you care so much," she says, her eyes locked on mine.

You existed.

Christ, I'm pathetic. This isn't just about making amends for past mistakes. There's something about *her* that had me tied in knots when I thought she was missing. Something about *her* that had me getting on that plane.

I don't want to analyze that right now. Instead, I slide my hands under her short skirt and skim my fingers over wet lace. She lifts her hips, coming up onto her knees to give me a better angle to slide my fingers into her panties. "Maybe our time together won't be as bad as you imagine."

Fuck. She's so wet, and I'm half hard again just feeling her. I slide one finger inside her and she gasps, her sex squeezing tight around me, and then suddenly she's scrambling into the seat beside me.

She smooths down her skirt and I'm trying to figure out what the fuck I did to make her pull away when my driver opens the door. We've arrived at the back entrance of the hotel, and I had no idea we'd even gotten close.

I don't just lose my focus around her. I lose my mind.

CHAPTER NINE

Janelle

CADE CLIMBS OUT OF THE CAR and offers his hand to help me.

Can a person die of lust? Because I might. I can still taste him on my tongue and my head is filled with the low sounds he made while I went down on him. When he slid a finger inside me, I thought I might come right then and there. The sight of the driver walking around to open Cade's door was the only thing that stopped my spontaneous combustion.

There's a bellman waiting for us by the back entrance. "Welcome back, Mr. Watts," he says with a nod. I notice he never acknowledges me by name, but I'd bet money he knows who I am.

"Thank you." Cade pulls me closer as he tucks my hand under his arm.

I shouldn't overthink this, but I'm struck by the difference in him—the stark contrast between this Cade and the one who found me in the club. That Cade was the irritated bodyguard. This Cade holds me close in a way that is warmer and more possessive.

We're led through the service entrance and to the housekeeping elevator. Cade's steps are long and purposeful, as if he wants us to be alone again as much as I do.

"Are you still planning to check out tomorrow, Mr. Watts?" the bellman asks as we file into the elevator.

"Yes, but we may need the room until mid-afternoon," Cade says. "I have a meeting in the morning."

"Where are we going tomorrow?" As soon as the words are out of my mouth, I want to snatch them back. *We?* I shouldn't assume there's a *we*. Maybe Cade plans to be done with me tomorrow. Maybe he—

"We're going home."

"Home?"

"You're staying at my place." Any softness that had found its way into his expression earlier leaves, and his face goes hard. "No arguments. There's too much we don't know."

He means we're returning to New Hope, but New Hope isn't my home. It's the place I stay when I'm trying to escape the loneliness of my real life. My life in LA. My fake life that's as empty and shallow as the people I called my friends. If Courtney and Jo had been real friends, I wouldn't have lost them as easily as I did my marriage.

New Hope is the place I go to pretend I can have all the things my brother found with Hanna. I'm not sure how I should feel about going there and staying with

Cade. A dull warning bell rings in the back of my mind, but I ignore it in favor of the warmth swirling in my belly.

It would be a mistake to want anything more from Cade than what he's offering. And what is he offering, exactly? Protection and maybe a few mind-blowing orgasms to pass the time. Is that enough for me?

The elevator dings, and Cade leads the way to our room and unlocks the door with his keycard. He walks straight to the couch where he had his makeshift bed. The pillow is on the floor and a blanket sits in a bunch on the coffee table, as if he kicked it there in his sleep. He lifts it, finding the note beneath and studying it for a beat.

"Fuck," he mutters, and his jaw tightens.

I don't want to lose what we had in the car. "I should have woken you," I blurt out. I don't know what I would do if I could go back, but I hate that I caused him so much worry.

"Yes. You should have. But *I* should have thought to look for a fucking note." He drags a hand through his short dark hair. "Fuck, fuck, fuck. You do something to me, princess. You make me . . ." He shakes his head.

"What?" I take the opportunity to turn the tables on him. "What do I make you?"

"Careless," he says, dropping the note back onto the end table. "Panicked. And really fucking bad at my job."

There's that word again. *Job.* It's a reminder I need. "Did someone hire you to protect me?"

"No."

"I don't understand why you're here, then. You protect people, sure, but you could be doing that at home. Doing the job you're paid to do."

He swallows. "Once I was pissed off at someone, and I didn't protect her like I should have. I promised myself I wouldn't make that mistake again."

There's more there, maybe something with Cara, but I decide not to dig. Not yet. Instead, I take the information for what it is—a reminder that this isn't about me—and wrap it like a flimsy barrier around my heart. It's not enough in terms of armor, but it's all I have against a man who strips me bare.

"You'll come home with me tomorrow?" he asks. His eyes are hot and hungry when he turns them on me, and with that flutter of anticipation in my belly, I make my decision. What he's offering might not be enough, but I'm going to take it, even if the price is my heart. "You'll stay at my place?"

"Suddenly I have a choice?" I'm teasing, but he stalks toward me.

"Not really, princess." He slides a hand into my hair and lowers his mouth until it's hovering so close I can almost taste him. "Don't argue with me, okay?" His lips brush across mine. Teasing. Sweet. "Just tell me you'll come. Tell me I'll have you with me."

Of course I'll come. Even if I didn't take the stalker situation seriously, there's the fact that Cade is doing me a huge favor by pretending to be my boyfriend. And even if neither of those held true, there's the way he's asking, and how desperately I want more of him.

"Yes," I whisper. "I'll come with you."

He grins. Holy shit that looks good on him. "You need sleep," he says.

"Didn't you brush me off with that line once already today?"

Dipping his head to nuzzle the side of my neck, he groans. "I'm not brushing you off, sweetheart." His hands skim down my sides and back up before he steps away. "I'm trying to be thoughtful."

Damn. He's unreal. "I couldn't possibly fall asleep."

"Why not?"

"Because I . . ." I nearly back out of that sentence, but he holds my gaze, demanding the rest. I take a breath, press my hand to his chest, and whisper, "Because I *ache.*"

His nostrils flare and his chest rises as he draws in a deep breath. "Tell me where." He rests a hand on my shoulder. "Show me."

"Everywhere." I lead his hand to drag across my breasts. "Here." Then lower until his fingers skim the low waistband of my skirt. "Down there."

As he curls his fingers into my skirt, he presses his mouth to mine.

Then his phone rings.

Cade tears his mouth away, cursing. "Hold that thought." He pulls his phone from his pocket and answers with a terse "Yeah?" but he never takes his eyes off me.

I slowly shimmy out of my skirt then pull my shirt overhead. I can't wear a bra with that one, so that leaves me in front of him in nothing but my panties. Holding his gaze, I lie on the bed and trail my fingertips over my bare stomach.

"Nothing?" Cade asks, and I feel a little bit of pride at the hitch in his gravelly voice.

I trail my fingers to the waistband of my panties and watch his nostrils flare. He licks his lips and I slide my hand lower, skimming my center through my panties. I can't believe I'm doing this, and yet it feels natural. He makes me feel bold. Uninhibited. He makes me the brazen woman my husband wished I would be. But I couldn't be like this with Tom. I was too self-conscious with him.

"Right. Got it." Cade swallows hard, and takes half a step toward me before stopping himself. "Okay. Yeah. I'll touch base before we fly. Thanks, brother." He punches at his screen then drops the phone to the end table before coming for me. At the side of the bed, he leans over me and kisses me hard.

When he pulls away, I'm breathless, and the ache between my legs has spread to consume every inch of me. He takes a step back. "Sorry. I didn't mean to interrupt what you were doing, but I had to kiss you."

"You didn't interrupt a thing."

He arches a brow and shifts his gaze to the lace between my legs. "I liked watching you touch yourself."

The words steal my breath. "Yeah?"

"Oh, yeah."

"I wasn't actually . . ." My cheeks burn. I was just trying to be sexy. Did he think I was going to masturbate in front of him?

"Why are you embarrassed now? I like watching you

in general, but the sight of you damn near naked on that bed, your hand between your legs, is one of the top two sexiest things I've ever seen."

"What's the other?"

The corner of his mouth twitches into a lopsided grin. "Do you have to ask?"

Maybe I shouldn't. Maybe it's Cara or someone else, and maybe I shouldn't want to know, but I do. I want to know everything about what turns Cade on. For as long as I get him, I want to be everything that turns him on and gets him off. "Tell me."

"The sight of you on your knees." His voice drops to a whisper even though we're all alone. "Your cheeks flushed and your mouth stretched around my dick while you took me deep."

"Oh." Wow. The mouth on this man. "So, it was . . . okay?"

He tilts his head and studies me as if he's trying to figure something out, but if he has a question, he doesn't ask it. Instead, he strips down to his boxer briefs and climbs onto the bed. He hovers over me, his weight on his arms. "You're nothing like I expected."

"Since I know what you expect of actresses, I'll take that as a compliment."

"I'm sorry if I was a dick when I found out about the cameras."

"And then a bigger dick when you found out about Matthew."

"Yes. That." Sighing, he buries his face in the crook of my neck. "I hate that motherfucker."

Giggling, I draw my knees up so they're each on

either side of his hips. He's hard again, and—thank you, sweet baby Jesus—his cock nestles between my legs. "Oh, I think everyone hates Matt at least a little. He's the devil."

He groans and cups one breast in his big hand. "I don't want to talk about Matthew Hailey right now."

I lift my hips off the bed and roll them experimentally. "What do you want to talk about?"

"Fuck, sweetheart. I don't want to talk at all." He kisses my neck then slides down my body, running hot open-mouthed kisses to my shoulder, across my collarbone, and to the valley between my breasts. "I just want to touch you, to hear you, to make you come."

When he sucks a nipple into his mouth, I arch off the bed and drive my hands into his hair. He keeps his cock pressed firmly between my legs and I rock against him, greedy with need.

"Tell me how to get you off tonight," he says. "Do you want my hands or my mouth?"

"More." I roll my hips again and moan. "Please."

He squeezes his eyes shut and grips my hips hard, stilling my movements. "Do you want to stay like this?" he says breathlessly. "Rub against each other and get off like a couple of teenagers?"

His words are almost as good as his hands, but I want more. I whimper, and he hears it.

"Tell me," he says.

"You're going to make me say it, aren't you?"

"There's nothing wrong with telling your lover what you need."

My lover. That is what I want. I want this man to be

my lover in every sense of the word. For as long as I can have him. I swallow hard and lock my gaze on his. "I need you inside me."

"*Christ*," he hisses, closing his eyes. "I want that too."

"So, why—" That's when it registers, and I nearly scream in frustration. "We don't have a condom?"

"Unless you've got one stashed somewhere," he says. "This wasn't exactly what I had planned when I came to LA." His eyelids are heavy, his lips parted. He rises onto his knees, positioning himself between my feet at the end of the bed. Slowly, he pulls off my panties and throws them to the floor. "Maybe I was wrong."

"About what?"

"I think we *should* talk." He slides a hand behind each of my knees, opening me to his greedy gaze.

"Talk? I thought . . ." I have to press my head back into the pillow as he traces the center of my exposed sex with one finger. My body pulses. Instinctively, I squeeze my legs together and he guides them wide again. "You're sure you want to *talk?*" I ask.

"I'm sure," he says. "Maybe I should tell you exactly what I'm going to do to you when I get you home. Maybe I should tell you all the ways I'm going to fuck you when I finally get the chance." His gaze flicks up to mine, and he watches my face as he slides two fingers inside me.

I cry out at the intrusion. It's too much at first and then just perfect as he slowly works his fingers in and out of me. "Yes," I whimper.

"I want you spread out on my bed—on your back with your ankles on my shoulders, then I'll roll you on your knees and see how deep you can take me."

I rock my hips into his hand and murmur "please," but I don't know what I'm begging for. More of his touch? More of his dirty mouth? The very scene he's describing?

"Some lazy night in, I'll fuck you on the couch. You'll straddle me, and I'll watch your tits bounce as you ride me. You have perfect fucking tits. I want to bury my face in them while you slide up and down my cock. I want to suck on them until you come."

He reaches up with his free hand, skimming my nipple with his rough fingertips, and my hips jerk. My body's on fire. I'm seconds from falling apart. "Cade."

"I'd need you in the shower too." His voice has gone hoarse, but he keeps talking as he fucks me with his fingers. "I'll push into you from behind, my hands on your breasts." He pinches my nipple then rolls it between his fingers. "I'd listen for your moans as I teased your nipples. Could you come like that? Or would you need me to touch you here?" He dips his head and flicks my clit with his tongue.

My body shudders under his touch, and he does it again—a single swipe of his tongue along my clit. And it's too much and not enough, and I want to scream in frustration because my body is climbing, ready for that fall, but I can't quite—

"Fuck, I love your taste." He wraps his lips around my clit and sucks, and that's when it happens. I scream. My hips buck. Every muscle in my body lets go.

But I don't fall. I fly.

* * *

Cade

"Where are you going?" Janelle reaches for me as I climb out of bed.

I mean to keep moving, to pull my jeans on and answer the door, but when I turn back to her, I have to pause for a minute.

The knock sounds again, but *damn.* I can't pull myself away from the sight of her.

"Who's at the door?" she mumbles, squinting against the morning sun.

Half her long, dark hair is still in a ponytail that's fallen to the side of her head and the other half is splayed across the pillow in every direction. Except for the thin white sheet tangled around her legs, she's nude, and I mentally catalogue every spot I touched last night, every place I tasted and want to taste again. Her lips are swollen from my mouth, and there's a faint trail of beard burn between her breasts.

Her hand goes to her hair. "Oh my God! I'm a wreck!"

I grin. "Total wreck." *And the most beautiful thing I've ever seen.*

Squealing, she treats me to a new view—her ass as she runs to the bathroom. "Just let me wash up."

Only after she shuts the door and I can hear running water in the sink do I finally pull on my jeans and turn back to the persistent knocking.

We spent the night sleeping and touching in cycles. Every time I woke, I was hungrier for her. I would have given my left nut for a condom. Once, when I woke to her rubbing her ass against my cock, I almost suggested we go ahead without. Which is only further evidence that she makes me lose my mind. Luckily, I came to my senses before the question could pass my lips.

After another round of knocking, I yank open the door and find Tom Comer in the hallway.

After last night, seeing him here is the worst kind of punch in the nuts. *"He was my husband first."*

Every muscle in my body coils with tension, but I keep my face blank. "What?"

He glares at me, his hands fidgeting at his sides. His hair's mussed and his he has dark circles under his eyes. "I need to talk to Janelle. She's not answering her phone."

Sometimes I wish I were an asshole. Because right now, an asshole would tell this piece of shit how it is. Something like, *She didn't have time to talk to you. She was too busy coming on my face.* I respect Janelle too much to say it, but it would feel really fucking good to see his reaction. I don't know much about Tom, and what I do know comes from his exchange with Janelle at the precinct and Janelle's insecurities in bed. Maybe it's not much to go on, but it's enough for me to be sure he doesn't deserve her.

He lifts onto his toes to look over my shoulder. "I

know she's here."

He shouldn't. No one is supposed to know—not our hotel and definitely not our fucking room number. I picked this hotel because I know the head of security and tipped the staff handsomely to keep our presence a secret.

"Just let me in," Tom says.

"Why?"

"Tom?"

I spin to Janelle standing behind me. Her face is shiny and freshly scrubbed. Her hair's been brushed, and it falls in soft waves down the back of her robe.

"There you are!" Tom steps into the room. I want to grab him by the neck and drag him back out, but I resist the urge and choose to study Janelle's reaction to him instead.

She's stiff, as if she's just as surprised to see him as I am. She looks from Tom to me and back to Tom. "What are you doing here?"

Tom turns to me. "May I speak with my wife alone?"

"She's not your wife anymore." I try for matter-of-fact, but the words come out like a growl from an angry dog.

He nods and returns his gaze to Janelle. "And I regret that every day."

Janelle winces. "Tom—"

"I told Bella this morning that I couldn't do it anymore," he says. "Knowing you're in danger has made me realize what really matters. I left her. I mean it this time. I won't let you go through this alone. Stay with me. Let me take care of you."

CHAPTER
TEN

Janelle

I BLINK AT TOM BEFORE TURNING TO CADE, whose expression has gone ice cold, a stark contrast to the warmth in his eyes just minutes ago.

Is this seriously happening? Maybe last night with Cade was some long, extended dream, and this is the part where the fantasy turns into a twisted nightmare.

"Janelle," Tom says, "what are you doing?" His frown is directed at where I'm pinching my arm.

Definitely not dreaming. I clear my throat. "Cade, could Tom and I speak in private? Please?"

When Cade turns his dark eyes on me, I realize I was wrong. There's no coldness in his expression. Instead, it's blank, and his eyes are vacant, as if he's thrown up a wall between his face and everything happening in his head. I won't let myself think about what might be happening in his heart.

"We just need a few minutes," I say.

"I need to head in to the precinct." Cade looks to

Tom and a hint of hardness returns to his jaw. "My guy Davis will keep an eye on things while I'm gone. He'll be waiting outside the door." He leaves it at that, and I'm not sure what the implication is. That Davis won't let me leave, or just a heads-up that he's supposed to be there?

"Davis?" I ask.

"You met him yesterday. I put him up in the room next door and have him on call."

"The babysitter," I mutter. "Right."

Something twitches in Cade's jaw, but he grabs a shirt from his bag. He pulls it over his head, covering all ninety feet of his bare, broad shoulders. "Have a nice . . . *talk*." He grabs his phone, wallet, and keys, and he's gone. And even though I'm the one who asked for privacy, even though I know I can't have this conversation with Cade looking on, I can't help but feel a tinge like I've been abandoned.

I don't turn back to Tom until the door clicks closed behind Cade. "What was that?"

Tom shifts from one foot to the other and shrugs. "I think he's mad about me coming here."

"Not Cade. *You.* What the hell do you think you're doing? Showing up like this? Saying those things in front of my—"

"Your *what*?" Tom asks.

Oh hell. That's a good question. "My boyfriend." I lift my chin, owning the lie.

"You still want me to believe you're with that guy? Come on, Elle. I know this city. I know the game you're playing. And I know you were at the HiLo with

Matthew Hailey last night. Doesn't take a genius to add it all up." He cocks his head and gives me that annoying *gotcha* grin before pointing to the seating area behind me. "And if I had any doubts, the sheets and pillows around the couch would give you two away."

I draw in a deep breath and exhale slowly. Cade may have shared the bed with me last night, but we never cleaned up the evidence of where he slept yesterday morning.

"You don't have to lie to me," he says. "I'm on your side."

"I'm not going to stand here and explain my relationship with Cade to you." Not that I could if I wanted to. I'd have to understand it myself first.

"Don't you understand? *That*"—he points to the couch again—"is the evidence that you two aren't sleeping together? It's a goddamn *relief*." Tom walks forward and takes my hand. "When he kissed you yesterday, I felt like he was ripping my insides out. You're mine, Janelle. I want you back." He dips his head, lowering his mouth to mine, but I step away before he can kiss me.

"No." *Fuckity fuck fuck fuck.* Why does he insist on playing games with my head?

Tom holds up his hands. "I get it. You've gone to all this trouble to convince Helen that you're with the cop so she won't boot you off the film."

"How do you know about Helen?"

"Bella's dad is friends with her and . . ." He shrugs. "People talk. But I get it. You're worried how it will look if you're suddenly with me again."

That hadn't even occurred to me. "You think that's my biggest worry?" I shake my head. "You had me believing you'd left her. I kissed you and started planning our lives together again. You made me look like a home-wrecking slut to the whole world."

"I'm sorry about how that unraveled. If I could do it over, I'd have gotten you somewhere private before kissing you."

I study the floor. He would have gotten me somewhere private—not he would have left Bella like he said he had. Not he wouldn't have lied. "If you really want to leave your wife, leave her. Get a divorce and make it final. Then—and only then—will we talk."

"If your plan is to come back to me once I have some divorce papers, why wait?"

That isn't my plan, but a week ago, it would have been. If Tom had shown me divorce papers, I would have been in his bed that night. And suddenly that seems so pathetic to me. This man broke my heart and my trust, and I would have gone back to him so easily just so he could do it all over again.

Things are different now. Not because of Cade and our non-relationship, but because of what my short time with him has made me feel. Even in his bossiest, most Neanderthal moments, Cade makes me feel special. Valued. Not just a possession to be protected, but a woman to be cherished.

I shake my head. "Don't put words in my mouth."

"Remember when we talked about having babies?" He tilts his head in that signature big-screen Tom Comer expression that makes all the fangirls swoon.

"I'm ready for all of that. We're meant to be together. The rest is logistics."

"You're married to another woman, and you're going to stand there and talk to me about *babies*?" My voice cracks on the word, as if years of him alternately promising and denying me that dream broke the word itself.

"I can't stomach the idea of some other man touching you, even if it's just for show."

"You need to leave." I press a hand to the ache in my stomach. "You've broken my trust too many times. If there's any future for us—and that's a big *if*—it won't start like this. Make your decisions. Do what you need to do, but do it without any expectation of what will happen between us."

He tucks his hands in his pockets. "Will you ever be able to forgive me?"

"I hope so." I step around him and open the door. "But forgiveness and trust aren't the same thing."

* * *

Cade

"Where's Janelle?" Gormong asks, when I step into his office.

I slide a Starbucks cup across his desk. "At the hotel. I've got Davis with her, though. She's covered."

Gormong takes a long pull of his coffee and studies

me. "Want to pretend you're not in a horrible mood and get down to business, or do you need to take a minute to share your feelings and shit?"

I grunt. "I'm not going to honor that with a response."

He lifts a shoulder. "Wife filled me in on the drama between your actress and her ex. And anyone with a pulse can tell there's tension between you two. I'm just saying we can talk if that's what you need."

I narrow my eyes at him. "No, you're saying your wife will be on your ass for all the details the tabloids aren't supplying."

"Harsh!"

"You can tell her that Janelle and I are fine." What a lie. We aren't fine. We aren't anything. Tom's appearance this morning was enough to jeopardize even our fictional romance, enough to remind me why I need to keep my distance.

"Fine?" Gormong grimaces. "You're sending me home with *fine*?"

"At least you're admitting your ulterior motives now."

The corner of his mouth twitches into a grin. "Hey, you can't blame me for trying. Happy wife, happy life, right?"

I wouldn't know. "So the case," I say, changing the subject none-too-subtly. "Where are we with security footage at Janelle's condo?"

He shifts uncomfortably. "You're not gonna like it."

"It's gone?"

"On the night before she returned—and the night

Courtney went missing—there's a gap of a few hours in the footage, as if someone went in and erased it. They're giving us a list of employees who have access to the digital files, and we'll start interviews."

"The more people you talk to, the harder it's going to be to keep this quiet. People will start asking questions. The media would love to get their hands on all the details of this story."

"I know. And since the HiLo is requiring we get a warrant before they'll share their security footage of the night Courtney disappeared, we're at a bit of a standstill with that line of the investigation. In the meantime, the more we learn, the uglier this case gets."

"What do you mean by that?" Then it hits me. The question I haven't asked. The question I've put out of my mind because to stay sane I have to believe that Janelle isn't in that kind of danger. But I know now. Even before I ask. "What were the results of the rape kit?"

Gormong's mood shifts in an instant. He drags a hand over his face and studies his desk.

"Fuck," I whisper. "What did they find?"

He swallows hard. "Her exam showed no internal injuries, but there were traces of semen. It can't be from her husband, because he'd been out of town for the previous week. We have samples being analyzed now, and when we have DNA information, we'll see if we can find a match in the database."

I grab my phone. I want to rush back to the hotel. I was so pissed that she wanted to talk to Tom alone that I got out of there as fast as I could. I shouldn't have left her. She should be with me. Until we have a suspect, everyone who *glances* at her is a potential rapist in my eyes—even a man she was once married to.

I don't care if he was her husband. They can have their conversation with my guy in the room.

I dial Davis, and he answers on the first ring. "Yes, sir?"

"Is Tom Comer still there?"

"No, sir. He left shortly after you."

I lean back in my chair and exhale, ignoring the questioning look Gormong throws in my direction. "And Janelle?"

"Safely in the room. Just ordered room service. She requested I join her for coffee, but I declined."

"Take her up on it," I say. There aren't many people in this world I trust completely, but Davis is one of them. "I'd feel better knowing you were with her until I can get back."

"Yes, sir."

When I end the call, Gormong clears his throat. "Tom Comer was with Janelle when you left?"

"Butt out," I mutter.

"My wife said that guy did a real number on your girl. Fucked around. Seemed to think he was entitled to do so. He did a couple interviews where he strongly implied that their marriage was falling apart because she was cold in bed."

None of this comes as a surprise to me. The night of the Halloween party, she told me it was the first time she'd had an orgasm from a man going down on her. The next day, when I found out who she was, I all but accused her of lying about that. But now I know I was wrong, and I have no doubt that any and all of her sexual insecurities come from her asshole ex-husband. What Gormong's telling me now only makes me regret that I didn't punch him in the face when I had the chance. "Comer's a tool," I mutter.

"Sure you don't want to talk about it?"

I scowl. "What did we find out about Courtney's memory loss?"

He sorts through a stack of papers on his desk and shakes his head. "Blood test was negative for Rohypnol."

"GHB? Ketamine?"

"Both negative," he says. "There were traces of Ambien in her system, but since she has a prescription for that and takes it regularly to help her sleep, it's not clear that it was administered by the perp. It's gained popularity as a rape drug, so that's our best guess at this point."

"How's she holding up?"

Gormong lifts his hands, palms up. "As well as should be expected. She's spooked and shaky. Emotional. The doctor gave her something for anxiety and let her go home with her husband. We're having patrol officers keep an eye on all the girls' residences, but there's been no suspicious activity that they've noted."

"So we know that her last memory is at the HiLo. But at some point after she arrived at the club, or possibly after she left, she was abducted without anyone noticing, tied up, causing the ligature marks on her arms, and then raped. The rapist leaves behind DNA evidence, but is able to execute every other part of his plan without a trace." I shake my head. "It doesn't add up."

"Which part?" Gormong asks.

"Let's remember that we're presuming this is the same guy who was able to get into Janelle's building undetected. Why would someone so careful in every other aspect be careless enough to leave behind DNA evidence? What does he want with them? Why send out all these letters? What's the end game?"

Gormong taps his pen on his desk. "All very good questions, but I don't think we should rule out the possibility that this is some basic sicko with a sexual fetish for these girls. Maybe all his caution went out the window when he actually had Courtney. He got too excited and careless."

I shake my head. Everything else is too calculated. Carelessness doesn't fit his MO. My stomach knots hard. "Or maybe it wasn't carelessness at all. Maybe this sick fuck wanted to make sure we know what Courtney can't remember."

"You think he *wants* the police to know he's a rapist?"

I shake my head. "Not the police."

Gormong's jaw goes tight. "The girls," he mutters. "Maybe this isn't about getting them. Maybe it's about the chase. He wants them to be scared."

I stand. "I have to get back to Janelle. We're going back to Indiana today."

Gormong nods. "That's a good idea. I'll keep you in

the loop."

There's a knock on the door, and we look up to see a uniformed officer entering. "Sir," he says to Gormong. "The TV. You're going to want to see this."

Gormong and I follow him to the break room, where the TV is playing the local news. "And tonight," the newscaster says, "more about actress Courtney Ferguson's shocking and inexplicable abduction, and the details the police have kept secret until now. You'll want to know all about the trouble that has this actress, as well as the other actresses from the show *Roommates,* fearing for their safety. Tune in for all the details in the case of the Flower Stalker."

"I want to know who in this precinct has talked to the press," Gormong says, scowling at the screen. "And I want to know now."

* * *

Janelle

"Thank you for coming in." I pour two cups of the coffee I ordered from room service. "When you were in the hall like that, I felt like I had a guard dog."

Davis grins. "That's my job, ma'am."

"Cream or sugar?"

"Black, please."

I add cream to mine and then hand over his. "So how do you know Cade?"

"We were in the military together," he says. "And he worked for my security firm for a couple years before leaving LA."

I sip my coffee. "So you probably have some good stories, huh?"

His normally stoic expression cracks with his grin. "None he'd want me to tell you, ma'am."

"He's really a good guy. Isn't he?" I don't know what Davis knows about my relationship with Cade. Maybe he thinks we're a couple like everyone else and my question seems strange, but he takes it in stride.

"The best. I'd trust him with my life, my family's life. Not many men I can say that about."

"Do you know his family at all?" I ask, but before he can answer, my phone dings. My sister-in-law is requesting a video chat.

Davis nods at me to take it, so I swipe the screen to accept.

"Hanna!" Just saying her name makes me smile, or maybe it was last night with Cade that's responsible for the grin on my face. Even Tom's stunt this morning can't take away that kind of glow.

"So, you got a really creepy delivery this morning," Hanna says.

"Where? At your place?"

Hanna glances off-screen and nods. "Yeah. I found these flowers on the front porch."

"Flowers?" In the corner of the screen, I see my face go pale. "You got a flower delivery for me? At your house?" *Oh God. Please don't let this be what I think . .*
.

"Does this mean anything to you?" Hanna asks. "The card says, 'Loves me not.'" She swings the phone around and suddenly my screen is filled with the image of a bouquet of at least a dozen dead and withered daisies.

CHAPTER
ELEVEN

Cade

W HEN I RETURN TO THE HOTEL, someone calls my name. My old friend Patterson, the hotel's head of security, stands in a suit by the registration desk, hands tucked into his pockets.

Seconds ago, I was fantasizing about going back to the room. Janelle would tell me she told Tom to fuck off and then I'd get her naked. But the fantasy fizzles away when I see Patterson's tense expression. "What happened?"

"She's fine," he says. "Come with me."

I follow him to an office down a back hall, and when he opens the door, my gut turns to ice.

"These were delivered this morning," he says. He points to the giant arrangement of daisies on his desk. The ones that seem to be laughing at me. "I'm told the delivery man gave your room number and left. Since I have you and Miss Crane registered under an alias, the front desk thought it was a mistake when he saw the card. He was calling the flower shop when I happened by."

I part the flowers to read the card.

For Janelle. She loves me.

"Would your employee be able to identify the delivery guy?" I ask.

Patterson points to the wall of computers at the back of his office. "I've already pulled up the security footage."

I pull my phone from my pocket to call Gormong. I can't get Janelle out of this fucking town soon enough. But even as I start to dial, it rings in my hand, and Davis's face pops onto the screen.

"Hello?"

"What's your ETA?" he asks.

"I'm downstairs."

"You might want to get up here. Janelle got a delivery at her brother's house in New Hope today. She has her sister on video chat now. You're going to want to see this."

"On my way." I end the call and look at Patterson. "Get Gormong over here."

* * *

Janelle

I open my mouth to speak, but my throat is thick and my thoughts are scrambled. I need to tell Cade about this. I need to call him and get him back here as soon as possible. I need to tell Hanna and my brother about the stalker and the investigation. But mostly, I need to find out what this guy wants from me, because I won't allow him to torment my family.

"Hanna, don't touch it, okay?" I say.

The lock on the door clicks, and Davis returns from the hall with Cade by his side.

"What is it?" Hanna asks. "You're freaking me out, and so are these flowers. What's going on?"

"Probably nothing." I hate lying to my sister-in-law, but I can't do much more until I'm allowed to talk about the investigation. I motion Cade over as I tell Hanna, "But we should take it seriously. Just in case it's a threat or something. Will you put it on the screen again so Cade can see?"

Hanna's eyes go wide, and she smiles. "Cade's there?"

"Um, yeah. He came out to be with me." I have to keep my explanation simple because I'm such a shitty liar. People say actors are great at deception, but when I act, I become someone else. I see the world the way they see it. Feel the way they feel. Acting and lying to your family aren't even in the same hemisphere.

"So, he's forgiven you? Because when I saw him at Brady's, he seemed pretty—"

"Hanna," I say firmly.

"Right. We'll talk later." She bites back her grin and adjusts her phone so the screen is filled with dead flowers.

Cade stands behind me and mutters a curse.

"What?" Hanna says. "What aren't you telling me?"

"Janelle has a stalker," Cade says, and I spin on him in surprise. "The daisies are his calling card."

I cock my head at him. "I thought we couldn't . . ."

"It's about to be all over the news," he says, his face grim. "Someone leaked the details of the investigation."

"A stalker?" Hanna says. "Do you know who it is?"

"I promise to fill you in later, okay?" I say.

"I'm going to send an NHPD officer to the house to get those flowers," Cade tells her. "He'll probably need to ask you a few questions about the delivery, too."

"Okay." Hanna's face is pale. "If it will help."

Cade nods. "Thanks."

"Talk soon, Han," I say, and before she can reply, Cade taps the screen to end our session.

"Fuck," he growls.

I sink into the couch. "You can say that again."

"I'll be in the hall," Davis says.

Cade lifts his chin in Davis's direction. "I'll debrief you in a few."

As the door clicks closed behind Davis, I try to figure out which Cade is pacing in front of me. The tender, warm lover who spent the night touching and tasting every inch of me? Or the cold, robotic bodyguard who finds me more an annoyance than an object of affection?

"He's screwing with our heads," he mutters. "Fucking psycho wants us to know you can't hide from him. Screwing with our heads."

I reach for his hand, and he flinches. *Okay, then. Hello, Mr. Bodyguard.*

"How did Tom know where to find you this morning?" he asks.

I shake my head, trying to keep up with the change of subject. "Tom?"

"He showed up at the fucking door to the hotel room where no one is supposed to find us. How did he know?" he asks between clenched teeth.

I cross my arms. This isn't just cold bodyguard Cade. This is *asshole* Cade. I stare at him, trying to figure it out. Last night was good. We were talking and touching and there wasn't all this weirdness between us. It's like he's not even the same guy who held me and kissed me and made me feel special.

"He knew because I told him. He texted me yesterday, worried about where I was staying. I told him."

"You gave him the room number?"

"He offered to bring some clothes for me—something *you* never bothered with—but then I decided Jamaal could help with that and told Tom not to come after all." And I decided I didn't want Tom, of all people, coming to my rescue.

"Who else did you tell?"

"No one."

"You're sure about that? Because if your precious Tom is the only one who knew where you were, that's pretty damning."

I don't know what he's talking about, but I'm not interested in trying to get an explanation out of him when he's in this mood. I turn on my heel, done with this conversation.

"Where are you going?" Cade calls to me.

"I need a shower."

"Good. We should get to the airport."

"Absolutely not." I point to my phone. "You saw that, didn't you? He delivered dead flowers to my brother's house trying to get to me. I'm not going to put his children in danger by going back there."

"He sent flowers here too," he says. "Live ones to be delivered to *this room* with a note with your name. *She loves me,* they say. They just never made it past the front desk."

A sharp chill, like a shard of ice, scrapes up my spine. "I thought no one knew I was here."

"No one but Tom?"

I flinch—not because I believe for a second that Tom has anything to do with this, but because of the venom in Cade's voice. As if I'm responsible for this on some level. "You think *Tom* sent those flowers? Broke into my apartment? *Kidnapped Courtney?* Seriously?"

"I'm just stating the facts. He knew where you were staying, and so did the person who sent the flowers." His face softens a little. "I don't know if Tom's behind this. I only know it would be easier to keep you safe at home."

There's that word again. *Home.* "I'm staying in LA."

"Can you at least be honest and admit why you're staying here?" He takes a step toward me, then seems to reconsider and stops, shoving his hands in his pockets. "Tom wants you back."

"So he says." I lift one shoulder in a shrug.

"You're going to stay in LA," he says. "You're going to sit and wait for him to divorce his wife so he can break your heart all over again."

Something inside me snaps, and I stride across the room to stand in front of him until we're inches apart. Craning my neck, I stare up at him and harden with every passing second. "You think you know me? Because, what, you lived in LA once? Because Cara Fray's a selfish bitch who broke your heart? And now you think you can sit there and play judge and jury to my life and my decisions?" I poke him in the chest. "Well, you don't. You don't know shit about me or my life or my mistakes. I already apologized for getting you involved in this, and I didn't ask you to come here. That was your choice. *Staying* was your choice. I've never asked anything of you, so you can just leave now."

I don't know what I expect—for him to grab his bag and head out the door, for another lecture about Tom or my decision to stay in LA—but it isn't this. I don't expect his lips to crush against mine or his hands to tunnel into my hair. I don't expect a kiss that is more teeth than tongue or for him to yank my body hard against his and hold me so tight I might actually believe he's afraid of losing me.

The moment my brain seems to register all of this, he releases me. He's breathing hard, and there's something in his eyes I want to believe is torment.

"I know it was my choice," he says softly. "And it was the right one." His thumb skims over my bottom lip and his eyes follow it. "Take your shower. We'll talk after."

* * *

Cade

"Well, fuck," Gormong says. He folds his arms and stares at the bouquet of daisies in Patterson's office. Patterson just left, giving us the room so we could discuss the case freely. "Is it a threat? Healthy and happy is LA, and the dead flowers are in New Hope? Is he trying to say something bad is going to happen to her if she goes back there?"

"Wouldn't he want her to think that? What better way to keep her here?" I exhale slowly. "Fuck if I know, but I hate the idea of her staying in this fucking town."

"We've got officers interviewing people at the flower shop now, and we're working with New Hope PD to interview the florist there. How often do people buy bouquets of daisies? Someone will remember something about this guy."

Something tells me our perp didn't show his face that foolishly, but I don't say so. "You need to call in Tom Comer. Question him about this."

Gormong is shorter than I am, but he manages to give the impression of looking down his nose. "Pardon me?"

I set my jaw. "These were delivered to the front

desk, and the guy gave our room number. Nobody but Tom knew where we were."

"I knew. Davis knew. Patterson knew."

"That's different."

Gormong shakes his head. "You want me to question an acclaimed actor for stalking a woman who clearly wants him back?"

Those words are a punch in the gut, and I have to set my jaw against the blow. "I do. Don't treat me like some irrational civilian. He's the most likely suspect here."

Gormong's face softens. "I'm sorry. I don't mean to be a dick, but you have to look at this from my perspective. You're asking me to believe that the guy who happens to be the biggest threat to your relationship is also a suspect in this case? Tom Comer? A psycho. A stalker. A rapist."

I flinch. "I know how it sounds, but this isn't about jealousy."

"The fuck it isn't. Cade, you hate the man. It's all over your face when his name comes up."

"I hate him," I say. I'd gladly shout it from the rooftops. "But that's not what this is about."

"Really? You're going to tell me you don't hate him because of what he did to Janelle. You don't hate what he means to her?"

"I don't like him, but this is simple logic. The person who sent these flowers knew what room we were in. Tom knew what room we were in."

"And Tom kissed your girl."

"She's not my girl," I grumble.

Gormong lifts a brow. "Say what now?"

"She isn't mine." I sigh. Gormong needs to know the truth. "Our relationship is a convenient cover-up for her mistake with Tom. She was up against a morality clause in a contract and at risk of losing a role. There is absolutely nothing between us." The last part feels like a lie, but I don't take it back. I shouldn't have kissed her, but I loved the way she stood up to me. I loved that she lifted her chin and told me, in so many words, to fuck off.

"Well, you could have fooled me." His eyes wrinkle in the corners as he studies me. "Pardon me for saying so, but a fake relationship to fool the media? That doesn't sound like you."

I have to agree with that. Letting jealousy fuck up an investigation doesn't sound like me either, but my gut tells me Gormong might be right about that. "Faking a relationship gave me an excuse for me to stay close while this investigation plays out."

His face goes sad as he studies me. "This is about Cara. When are you going to forgive yourself for that?"

I ignore his question along with the pity in his eyes and circle back to the subject at hand. "I'm not claiming to be objective, but if Tom wasn't a celebrity, you'd have him in there in an instant."

"I'll speak with him," Gormong says reluctantly. "But we're talking about a suspect who has hacked into surveillance systems and broken into a high-security condo. I don't think it's out of the realm of possibility to think he might have been able to find your hotel room." Gormong's phone rings and he holds up a finger, indicating for me to wait as he takes the call. "Yeah? . . . When? . . . Fuck. No. Send someone over there. I'll be back soon. Okay. Thanks."

I arch a brow as he hangs up. "So?"

"Jo and Courtney each got a bouquet of daisies this morning as well."

"Dead or alive?" I ask.

"Both. Each woman received one of each." Gormong exhales heavily and snaps his phone back into the clip at his belt. "I need to get going. Are you still planning to head back home today?"

"She won't go. After the flowers were delivered to her brother's house, she's too worried that going back there will put her family in danger."

Gormong tilts his head and studies me. "What are *you* going to do?"

"I'm staying." It's not a question for me. I can't go back to New Hope while she's here.

"You're staying in LA with your fake girlfriend? Don't you have to get back for work? Your *real* life?"

I sigh heavily. "I made arrangements for some time off. I can't leave her."

I can practically hear him mentally questioning how "fake" my relationship with Janelle really is, but he's smart enough not to do it out loud. "You have a place to stay?"

"I'm working on it. I'll let you know."

When Gormong leaves, I head back to the room. Janelle is out of the shower and dressed in the same clothes she wore the morning I arrived. The hotel laundry services must have brought them back to the room, and I feel like a world-class dick for not thinking about getting her some clothes and basic necessities the day I picked her up from the station. *Asshole ex-husband: 1, Asshole fake boyfriend: 0.*

"I'm done in there," she says, motioning to the bathroom. "If you need it."

Her hair hangs in wet locks down her back, and I have to fight the urge to comb my fingers through it, to hold it in my fist as I lower my mouth to hers again. I still can't believe I kissed her earlier. I thought my injured pride would prove useful for something, but nothing can help me resist the irresistible.

But *fuck*, I can't stop thinking about what she said to me the morning after our first night together. I all but accused her of being an adulteress and she said, "He was my husband first." Those words have haunted me through every second of our time together here. *"He was my husband first."* That sentence was proof to me that I needed to stay away from her. It was as if she believed she had some right to him because she'd been his wife before Bella, and I told myself she was all the worst things that come out of Hollywood. It was what I needed to believe. But my reaction to those words was more than that. There was also such a great sense of loss in them that I knew just how much he still had a hold on her. Or I should have known. But apparently, I let myself forget.

"What did you tell Tom this morning?" I ask.

"What?"

"He came here because he wants you back. What did you tell him when I left?"

"I . . ." She tilts her head, studying me. "Why do you care? Because if you're still trying to convince me that he's the one who sent those flowers—"

"I just want an answer, princess. It's not so hard."

She swallows, her pink tongue darting out to wet her lips. "I told him we could talk once his divorce was final."

"You're going to go back to him." It's not a question. It's me trying to come to terms with a reality I never should have forgotten. She didn't deceive me like Cara did. She told me up front. *"He was my husband first."* I shouldn't care. But I do.

"I didn't say that." She rubs her arms, as if this conversation is making her cold. "I told him he needed to make a decision about his marriage independent of what happens between us." She stands and walks over to the kitchenette to make herself a cup of coffee.

"Are you still in love with him?"

She freezes, one hand on the coffee pot, and turns back to me, pain all over her face. "Does it matter?"

"Yes." I take a step forward and then stop myself. I can't go to her. Even if her answer is *no*, I have to put an end to what we started last night, and what I foolishly continued by kissing her this morning. Being with her muddles my thoughts, and if I'm going to protect her I need to be on my A-game.

"He was my husband," she says. "I did love him. Maybe part of me still does. But it's not the same."

"Because he's married?"

She studies me for a long time before abandoning the coffee pot and turning to fully face me. "Because when someone hurts you, they change you."

"But you didn't tell him no? You didn't refuse his request to have you back."

"I'm here, aren't I?"

"No and *not right now* aren't the same thing."

She tears her gaze from mine. "I don't understand what you want from me."

I want to know why she didn't tell him to fuck off. I want to know why she didn't slam the door in his face and tell him there wasn't a chance of reconciliation. I want to understand why she would even consider letting him hurt her again. But I don't say any of that because I've already pried more than I have the right to. So I say, "I want you to go back to New Hope with me."

"I can't. And I've already made arrangements with Nate to use his house here. He's almost never there, but Jamaal's still on retainer and will help with security." Wincing, she motions to the door. "But don't let me slow you down. Go catch your plane or whatever."

"I'm not going back without you."

"Cade . . ." She blows out a long breath. "Listen, I appreciate that you want to protect me. Though I may not understand it completely, I do appreciate it. But I'm a grown woman, and I get to make my own decisions. Today, my decision is to stay as far away from my family as possible. I don't expect you to understand that, but it's what I have to do."

"I do understand," I say. I fist my hands at my side to fight the instinct to go to her, to touch her. "I still think we're being manipulated, that this guy wants you to stay in LA and sent those flowers to Nate and

Hanna's for that reason, but I do understand why you don't want to be close to them while you wait this out."

"You do?"

I nod and shove my hands into my pockets. "I would do the same thing."

"Oh."

"You still need a pretend boyfriend, right? To keep your part in the film? I'll stay with you at your brother's, get Davis to help with security, and we'll take it one day at a time."

"You're staying with me? As my boyfriend?" The confusion on her face threatens to tear my gut in two, reminding me again what a mistake it was to kiss her.

I swallow hard. "This isn't about sex or what happened between us last night. In fact, last night was—"

"Please don't call it a mistake."

My stomach pitches. She says she doesn't understand what I want from her, but I have to say that goes both ways. She just admitted that she's considering going back to her ex-husband, and yet she stands there and tells me not to call last night a mistake.

"If you call it a mistake," she says, lifting her eyes to meet mine, "it will make me feel like trash."

I shove my hands deeper in my pockets, fighting an internal war between not hurting her and not leading her to believe our relationship is anything more than an arrangement. But the vulnerability in her eyes begs me for the truth, and I hear myself say the words before I can decide if I should. "Touching you was only a mistake because it makes not touching you that much harder."

CHAPTER TWELVE

Janelle

IT SEEMS LIKE THERE ARE a thousand loose ends to tie up before we can leave the hotel, and the sun hovers low on the horizon as we ride to my brother's Hollywood home.

Davis drives, and Cade and I sit in the backseat along with our new constant companions, Tension and Awkward Silence. Only, this is Cade, so I can't decide if this companion is Sexual Tension or her asshole doppelgänger, Angry Tension.

Cade's hands grip his knees, and his gaze is fixed on some point beyond his window. He offered to make arrangements with Officer Gormong so I could get back into my condo and get some clothes, but I told him that wouldn't be necessary. I lived at Nate's house for a while after my divorce, and when I bought my condo, I left more in my room at Nate's than I took with me.

When Davis pulls past security and into the circle drive, I'm filled with the bittersweet emotions I've come to associate with this monstrosity. This is Nate's house now, but before that it was my father's. He left it to Nate when he died, and my brother and I have filled it with good memories—laughter, friends, the memories of his epic fall into love with Hanna. Before that, it was a symbol of the life our father chose over us—the new wife, the new children, and the career that was forever and always prioritized over his "old" life.

"Are you okay?" Cade asks, and I realize I'm still just staring and Davis has turned off the car.

"Yeah." I force a smile. "I'm great."

"Are you sure about that? You're looking at that place like it's haunted and you're terrified of ghosts."

That's not so far from the truth. "This was my father's house. He left it to Nate when he died."

"You lost your father?" He draws in a ragged breath. "I'm sorry. I had no idea. But I guess I should have. Your father was . . ." He pauses, as if searching his memory for the name. "Dritts Crane, right? The producer?"

"That's right." I stare at the front door as if he might appear there. We didn't visit often, but when we did, we always left feeling like his two greatest disappointments. He'd stand in that doorway, watching the car as his driver took us back to Mom's. Son-of-a-bitch rarely bothered to drive us himself. "Don't apologize," I tell Cade. "My father was an asshole. Our relationship was so screwed up, I'm not even sure I have the right to grieve."

Cade settles his hand on my thigh, and I distract myself from my thoughts by memorizing the way the heat seeps through the denim of my jeans, how small I feel under his touch. "Sure you do. You have every right to your grief. And if your relationship with him was troubled, you need it that much more."

When I lift my eyes to his, I see a sadness there that can only be explained by a common understanding. Cade's so strong—so solid and steadfast—it's easy to forget that he's a man who bleeds like any other, who's been hurt like any other. At least I hope that's easy to forget, because if I could, maybe, just maybe, I could resist him.

"Don't look at me like that," he murmurs, his gaze dropping to my lips. He grazes a thumb over the bottom one. It seems like his favorite spot, as if it's the one part of me he allows himself to touch.

"Look at you like what?"

"Like you want me to kiss you."

My tongue darts out to wet the spot he just touched and catches the corner of his thumb. "Why not?"

"Because, princess." He pulls his hand away and puts on that bodyguard face I've come to hate. "When I kiss your mouth, I like it. Then I remember how much I like kissing you in other places."

With that, he climbs out of the car. *Well, damn.*

Mutely, I follow him up the steps and slip in front of him to unlock the door.

"Auntie Elle!" a tiny voice shouts before I can push the door open. The greeting is followed by another voice shouting, "Auntie! Auntie! Auntie!"

My adorable little nieces toddle through the living room in their PJs and wrap themselves around my legs.

Laughing, I sink to the floor and let them climb onto my lap, my eyes filling with tears. I used to think that phrase "light of my life" was so trite and meaningless, but Sophie and Josie and their half-brother, Collin, are that for me. They're the light when the world gets too dark and heavy. They're everything that is good and hopeful, and any time I feel down, just looking at their faces shows me the path from the darkness.

And clearly I've had an emotional weekend, because seeing these doll faces shouldn't make me get quite so dramatic.

"Auntie cry!" Sophie wipes a tear from my cheek and presses a kiss to the wet spot.

"I'm just so happy to see you," I whisper, looking up to see my brother, his arms wrapped around his beautiful wife as they watch their precious girls snuggle into me.

"We wanted to surprise you," Hanna says, her eyes cutting to Cade. "I hope you don't mind."

"'Prise!" Josie says. "'Prise, Auntie!"

Somewhere in the mix, Cade moved to the back of the foyer, and now he stands in the shadows like the bodyguard he's determined to be.

"Cade," Nate says, with a nod in his direction. There's a tightness to my brother's jaw. He always liked Cade before, but apparently that's changed. *Completely your fault, Janelle.* If I'd been honest with Nate from the beginning, he'd see Cade for the saint he is.

"Nate," Cade says in return.

"When did you get in?" I ask to fill the silence. My

real question is, *When are you leaving?* My whole purpose for staying in LA was to keep this psycho as far as I can from Nate and his family. But since my father left this house to Nate, not me, I don't exactly have the right to ask them to leave.

"Maybe half an hour ago?" Hanna says. "It's past the girls' bedtime—even in this time zone—but I promised they could stay up for *one hug* before going to sleep. Get your hugs, girls. It's bedtime!"

There's a brief chorus of whining as the girls wrap their arms around my neck one last time, but their protests are short-lived, and they take their mom's hand and follow her up to bed.

"I'd love a beer," Nate says, turning to me. "You up for a drink?"

"Sure."

"I'll be right back down." Hanna gives a pointed look to her husband. "One drink and then *we* should be getting to bed too." Clearing her throat, she gives a not-so-subtle head tilt in the direction of me and Cade. "Bad enough to show up unannounced."

She heads up the stairs, and Nate, Cade, and I head into the kitchen. I open the fridge and am grateful Jamaal insisted on stocking it before we arrived. That man always proves useful for more than his intimidating demeanor.

I grab a couple of beers for the guys and a bottle of wine for myself. I get to work on the cork while Cade starts opening cabinets to find a glass.

"Glad to see you're making yourself at home," Nate says, and I'm not sure if he's being begrudgingly sincere or sarcastic. Judging by the tension in Cade's shoulders, he's not sure either.

"The glasses are in the far right cabinet," I tell Cade, pointing.

"Will Hanna want anything?" Cade asks.

"She's pregnant," Nate says with a completely unnecessary scowl.

"He meant water or something." Joining my brother at the center island, I give him a hard elbow nudge and my best *stop being a dick* glare.

He draws in a breath and says, "Milk. When she's growing my babies, she likes milk before bed."

"Please and thank you," Hanna says, joining us in the kitchen. "Nate, quit scowling at Cade."

"I'm the brother," he grumbles. "Scowling is my job."

Hanna rolls her eyes then redirects her focus on us. "Sorry for showing up unannounced. Nate saw the story about this Daisy Stalker online and insisted on seeing for himself that you are okay."

"I'm fine. See? Still in one piece." I hold out my arms and glance down at my body.

"I don't like any of this," Nate says. "How long has this asshole been sending you letters?"

"I've been getting them for a few weeks. Everything just kind of came to a head when I got back to LA."

My brother looks at Cade. "Is this guy dangerous?"

Cade pours a glass of milk and hands it to Hanna. "I believe he is," he says. "We honestly don't know much. He's covered his tracks almost too perfectly. In every way except . . ."

"Except what?" Hanna asks.

Cade takes a deep breath and studies me. I can tell by the look in his eyes that he's not sure how much he should say.

"You can say anything in front of Nate and Hanna that you'd say to me," I say.

"We have a couple leads we're working with now," he says carefully. He's obviously trying to frame this in the most optimistic light possible. "The flower shops, for starters."

"You said he's covered his tracks perfectly *except*," I say. "What's the *except*?"

He drags a hand over his face, and my stomach sinks. "Courtney's exam. There were traces of semen."

"She was raped," Hanna says. Her face is sheet white, and she presses her free hand to her stomach as if to protect the child growing there.

Cade watches his beer as he rolls it between his hands, his jaw tight. He doesn't want to talk about this, but he's doing it for me. "We're running the results of the sample through the offender database. If we're lucky, we'll find a match."

"And if there's no match?" Hanna asks. "If this guy hasn't ever been caught before?"

Cade lifts his eyes to mine, and I know without him saying that he's not optimistic. "He's escalating, and we're watching. The police have guys on every angle of this case."

Nate, who's been ominously silent until now, turns to me. "I want you to come back to New Hope."

I fold my arms. "No."

"You're being stubborn and ridiculous," Nate says. "I only want you safe, and I can't believe we're even having this conversation."

Cade grunts. "Welcome to my day."

"It's safer at home," Hanna says.

I lift my chin. "But it's not my home. I'm staying here. And until this guy is caught, I'd prefer those precious girls to be as far away from me as possible." Hurt flashes over Hanna's face, so I sigh and squeeze her hand. "Try not to worry. Cade's agreed to stay. He's taking good care of me."

Nate grunts. "Yeah, I've seen the pictures." He narrows his eyes at Cade. "How are you going to see the bad guy coming if you're too busy groping my sister?"

"Nate!" I screech, and at the same time, Hanna smacks him in the arm. When I straddled Cade and stuck my tongue down his throat while the photographers flashed their cameras, I hadn't been thinking of what my brother would think of Cade touching me like that. Or how he'd feel about said touching once I told him about how this mess all started.

In fact, I'd intended on telling Nate the truth the next time I saw him in person, but it might be easier for Nate to leave me in Cade's protection if he continues to believe the story we're selling.

Cade responds before I can. "We're hoping we can have a break from the cameras while we're staying here. It will be good to have a few days of privacy."

I study him for a long, stuttering beat of my heart

while I try to figure out if he means that. At no point today has my brain ventured far from his words at the hotel, and I circle back to them now.

"Touching you was only a mistake because it makes not touching you that much harder."

I've dissected that sentence and analyzed it from every angle, never sure what to make of it, never sure what I should expect from him while we're here. Then he said something similar before we got out of the car.

"When I kiss your mouth, I like it. Then I remember how much I like kissing you in other places."

In other words, he still wants me, but he doesn't plan on doing anything about it. As frustrating as that thought is, thinking about Cade wanting me—despite everything—makes the butterflies in my belly do a victory cheer.

Hanna clears her throat. "Come on, Nate. Let's give the lovebirds some of that privacy they're looking for." She grabs him by the wrist and tugs him toward her.

Nate gives me a pointed look. "We're not done talking about this."

"Good night," I say, and Hanna winks at me. God, I love that woman. She's the best thing that ever happened to my brother, and the best sister-in-law I could ask for.

Cade clears his throat. "I'll, uh, take our bags upstairs."

Oh, shit. Sleeping arrangements just got a little more interesting. "My room is at the top of the stairs and to the right." Our gazes lock for a beat before he nods and follows Hanna and Nate out of the kitchen.

I'm left alone with my thoughts and an untouched glass of wine. I try to wrap my mind around the new information about Courtney's exam, but I can't quite get it to sink in.

There's a rapist after me.

It's too surreal to process. I'm freaked out, yes, but not as much as I know I should be. This is something that happens to people in movies, not a trio of washed-up actresses, years out of the only roles anyone ever cared about.

I drain my glass and set it on the counter. I'm a few steps toward the stairs when I reconsider and go back for my glass and a bottle of wine. If I'm going to spend the night sharing a room with Cade and he's going to insist on keeping his distance, I'm going to need this.

When I get to my bedroom, Cade is sitting in one of the chairs, dressed in a pair of soft cotton pants and nothing else. His feet are propped on the ottoman and he's reading some action-packed thriller.

Sexy man. Bare chest. Book.

Damn.

"Hey," I whisper, closing the door behind me and refilling my glass of wine.

He marks his place and puts his book to the side. "Hey. I figured you'd want me to sleep in here. On the other hand, your brother kept looking at me like he wanted to cut my balls off, so maybe I'd be better off in the guest bedroom."

"I planned on telling him everything," I say. In two swigs, my glass is half empty again. Maybe it's not healthy to use alcohol as a coping mechanism for stress, but being healthy is the least of my worries at the moment.

Cade frowns. "About us?"

"I would have clued him in from the beginning if Matthew hadn't been so insistent. I don't keep secrets from my brother. At this point, I don't care what Matthew thinks or says. But then Nate started talking about getting me back to New Hope, and I decided he might be more comfortable with the lie." I bite my lip. "I don't know. Hanna's probably planning our wedding, so telling them sooner rather than later could do some damage control."

"It's up to you," he says.

I can't tear my eyes from where he's absently scratching his chest. I want my hands there. My mouth. I want to sleep wrapped in the safe heat of his muscles.

I drain my glass in an attempt to distract myself, but the wine seems to make the situation worse. Heat spreads through my belly and flips a switch that makes my hormones sing.

"But I'm guessing your brother knows you well enough to guess at the truth."

Those words tear me away from my man-chest ogling. "Excuse me?"

"You seem close," he says. "That's all."

"You're saying my brother knows me well enough to know a guy like you wouldn't want anything to do with someone like me?"

Arching a brow, he pushes himself out of his chair and crosses the room to stand in front of me. He takes the bottle of wine and my empty glass from my hands and sets them on the dresser, then he turns to study me. "I'm such an asshole," he mutters. Reaching out, he touches my shoulder and then drops his hand.

"But it's true," I whisper, hating the crack in my voice. "You wouldn't want to be with someone like me if we hadn't been thrown together out of necessity."

"I'm an asshole," he repeats, "but I'm not such an asshole that I can't admit when I was wrong, and I was wrong about you."

"Are you sure? I'm an actress. And we both know I'm not above lying to get my way." I'm not proud that I hired Matt, but somehow owning up to it makes me feel a little less shitty.

"I'm sure. It's been clear since I first arrived in LA and saw you at the precinct. I was watching on the other side of the glass while Tom talked to you, and I knew then . . ." He shifts awkwardly, then looks away. "I wish I could go back to the morning the pictures of us were first published. I said some terrible things."

"It looked bad," I say. "You had every reason to be angry."

"But you stand there thinking that a guy like me wouldn't want to be with a girl like you." He takes my hand, opens my fingers, and presses my palm flat to his bare chest. "Any guy—like me or way more fucking worthy than me—wouldn't just want you, sweetheart. He'd be lucky as fuck to have a chance."

My heart hammers wildly, and I'm thinking this would be the perfect moment for him to carry me to the bed, undress me, and make use of the condoms in the nightstand. Instead, he kisses my knuckles and releases my hand.

"I'll take the floor," he says. "I can sleep anywhere."

CHAPTER THIRTEEN

Cade

Wᴴɪʟᴇ Jᴀɴᴇʟʟᴇ ᴇxᴄᴜsᴇs ʜᴇʀsᴇʟꜰ to the attached bathroom to do whatever it is that women take so long to do before they can sleep, I find a spare comforter in the closet and use it to create a makeshift bed for myself.

Even though I knew days ago that I'd been wrong about Janelle, she still manages to surprise me. The way she collapsed onto the floor tonight so her nieces could climb on her lap—it tugged at something in my gut and didn't let go. Physical attraction is one thing, but I fucking *like* this woman. I like the way she laughs. The way little girl hugs can make her cry. The way she assumes the best about people, and the way she cares about her family.

I know she's going through a lot right now, and I know I've been a world-class dick through more of it than is fair. The least I can do is be honest with her. Do I wish she'd go back to Indiana? Yes. Do I wish she'd slammed the door in Tom's face this morning? *Abso-fucking-lutely.* But she shouldn't have to walk around thinking less of herself just because I'm frustrated that I can't have her.

I steal a pillow from the many piled up on her bed and toss it with my blankets on the floor. Then she walks out of the bathroom, and I nearly swallow my tongue.

She's dressed in tiny cotton shorts that show every inch of her long legs, and I can see the outline of her breasts through her thin tank top.

She looks from my blankets on the floor and back to me. "You're sure?"

I nod. "It's not a problem."

Her lips part, and she blows out a soft breath. Fuck, but I want to see her do that while I'm over her. While I'm inside her. I want to breathe her moans and taste her cries of pleasure.

"Okay," she says. "So . . . good night, I guess."

"Good night."

She climbs under the covers and waits for me to settle into my blankets before she shuts off the lights. The silence is thick and loaded with tension. Neither of us is ready for sleep.

"Are you ever going to tell me?" she asks after several minutes.

"Tell you what?" We should both be exhausted and falling asleep after the last few days, but sleeping down here with her so close will be easier said than done.

"What happened in your past that made you want to come here and protect me even when you thought the worst about me?"

I sigh heavily and roll to my side so I'm facing the bed. I don't like to dwell on my mistakes, but I find that I want to tell her this. "It was after I proposed to Cara and found out about Matt. I can't really explain what that time was like for me." I shake my head. "Never mind that. I'm glad I can't. I wouldn't want you to know how pathetic I was."

"She broke your trust," Janelle says softly.

"Yeah. For starters. I'd lived with her for months and thought what we had was real." Janelle shifts under the covers and I wish I were up there with her. I wish I could make out her features while still having the security of the darkness concealing mine.

"Maybe it was real," she says. "Just because it started as something else doesn't mean she didn't develop feelings for you along the way."

I follow her silhouette through the darkness as she reaches her hand off the side of the bed, searching for mine. Our fingertips graze.

"You're a catch, Officer Watts. Even the coldest heart could find herself falling for you."

And what about you? Are you falling for me? "Maybe, but in the end she didn't want to be with me. And it hurt my pride to know I'd been so thoroughly played."

Her fingers squeeze mine. "It hurt more than your pride."

"Yeah," I admit. This is easier than I'd have expected, opening up to her about something I've always considered my biggest embarrassment. "So I moved out, and in my anger I told her I was going to give interviews to all the journalists who wanted to know the details. I was going to let the world know who she really was—how shallow and manipulative she could be to get her way. I knew even when I said it that I'd never do that. Why would I want the whole world to know I was such a fool? What kind of man goes to bed with a woman every night, buys her a fucking engagement ring, and doesn't know she has no real attachment to him? But I threatened because I wanted to hurt her like she hurt me." I draw in a long breath, but my heart races like it happened yesterday. "She begged me not to give the interview. For a couple weeks, she'd leave me messages saying that she did have feelings for me but she wasn't sure what to do with them, that maybe we could work it out. More ploys. More efforts to manipulate me."

"Unless they weren't," Janelle says. "Unless she did want to work it out."

"It doesn't matter. At that point, she'd destroyed everything between us. And my pride was far too damaged for me to see her calls as anything other than manipulations. My heart, too." Cara was my first lesson that I can't trust my heart—in love or wounded, it fucks up my judgment. "But then she started calling and asking for help. She said this guy was stalking her, and she didn't feel safe. She wanted me to come stay with her because the police weren't taking it seriously. He hadn't done anything or said anything to indicate he was an obvious threat, and Cara had a history of overreacting in the face of overly enthusiastic fans.

And, of course, at this point I didn't believe a word that came out of her mouth."

"Oh, no," she whispers. "It was real. She really did have a stalker."

"Yeah. Crazy fucker, too. Just a kid on paper, but he was screwed up. I didn't believe her, though, and told her under no circumstances would I sleep under the same roof as her." I'm silent for a beat, remembering how angry I was and how I let that anger rule my decisions. "She was all alone at her house when the guy broke in and pinned her down on the bed." Just remembering how she looked afterward is enough to steal my breath. She was bundled up in a blanket at the station, the color drained from her face. I'm not sure she's ever forgiven me for failing her. I know I won't forgive myself.

"He raped her?" Janelle asks.

I shake my head, then remember she can't see me. "I'd asked one of the guys at the station to keep an eye on things. He was stopping by her place to check on her a couple times a day. He got there and heard her screaming, broke in, and yanked the guy off her. If he'd been five minutes later . . ."

"And you blame yourself."

"Yeah. I do. She wasn't asking me to be with her again at that point. She only wanted my protection, but I couldn't see anything but how she'd hurt me."

Janelle squeezes my fingers again, then laces them with mine. "It's not your fault."

"It is, though. She was different after that. We both were. When I found out the love of my life had only been using me, it broke something inside of me. And when she felt like she had no one when she needed someone the most, something broke inside of her."

"Cade . . ."

"No, listen. My father was an asshole. He was all about the almighty dollar and what it could get you. He worked constantly, building his company, and he hated his life. At night, he came home and made my mom feel like a piece of trash because *he* was working so hard, and what had she done?" I roll to my back and stare at the ceiling, at the dappled shadows cast by the moonlight filtering through the curtains. I didn't mean to talk about my father. I never talk about him. But Janelle's answering silence doesn't feel cold or judgmental. It feels like an open door, an invitation to share this with someone else who had a less-than-stellar father. "Mom left him when I was in high school, and Dad was only on the periphery of our lives until I graduated. He wanted me to take over the company when he retired, and I joined the military instead."

"What did he say?" she asks.

"He sneered at me, but I knew I didn't want to be like him. I wouldn't let my life be dictated by money or even some vague notion of success." I love the way Janelle's hand feels in mine—her soft skin and light touch. "I've spent my life priding myself on taking jobs that help people. That protect people. Maybe I'm not the world's best son or some amazing business mind, but I protect people. But in this case, when someone I loved needed protection, I couldn't see past my own hurt to do what I do best."

The rustling of sheets fills the room, but I don't realize what she's doing until she's on the floor with me, crawling under my blanket and resting her head on my chest. Her cheek is wet.

"You're crying."

"It's a sad story."

I told myself that from here on out, I was only touching her to comfort her, but now she's comforting me. And it feels damn good to be comforted. It's been a long time since I've felt like I could open up to someone.

"I hate that you blame yourself for that horrible experience of hers," she says. "I hate that you carry that around with you. Despite what you've told yourself, it's not your fault. You *saved* her by sending that officer to her house. And I hate what she did to you, but I understand why she asked you to move back in. It probably sounds terribly weak of me to admit, but I feel safe with you here. I'm glad you decided to come to LA, and I'm grateful you're staying."

I smooth her hair back and press a kiss to the top of her head. I've just handed Janelle a piece of myself, and instead of holding my breath to wait and see what she'll do with it, I realize I'm breathing easier because I know it's in good hands. "Thank you for listening. It's not something I talk about much."

"Any time." She repositions herself so she's lying on top of me, her head on my chest, her legs between mine. Our bodies are so close, the heat of her seeps into my skin, and it feels so good it literally hurts to not take more.

"Earlier today I—" I stop myself and squeeze my eyes shut against the ache of needing her. "My sister says Cara changed me, hardened me. These last few days with you are the first time I've seen that hardness as anything other than a blessing." I wrap my arms around her and roll us so we're on our sides, facing each other. "You said that Tom changed you when he hurt you, and I want to cut his dick off for that. You're precious." I can't make out her features, but I find her face in the darkness and trace the edge of her jaw and down her neck. "I don't ever want to be responsible for changing someone as amazing as you."

"You're afraid of hurting me?" I can practically hear the frown in her voice. "Is that why we're not using the condoms we finally have access to?"

My groan is edged with every bit of the agony I feel. "You're pure evil. We both know that's a bad idea after this morning."

"Because of Tom," she says.

"Don't get me wrong. There's a devil on my shoulder telling me I should just make you come so hard you can't remember his name."

"And what does your angel say?"

I press another kiss to the top of her head. "The angel reminds me I'm kind of an old-fashioned guy. I've never been interested in a physical relationship that has no future. I've never been a no-strings-attached type. I like strings and complications. Sex isn't simple for me. Until the night a sexy minx dressed as Catwoman asked me to leave her mask on, I was never interested in pursuing it with a woman whose future isn't tied up with mine."

"I'm sorry, I—"

I press a finger to her lips. "The angel says that if Asshole Tom is what you want—"

"Your angel calls him *Asshole* Tom?"

"Yes. Because angels don't like guys who hurt beautiful women. But if there's any chance Asshole Tom is what you want, you shouldn't fuck it up for some guy who lives in a different world. Your life here, your career—those things are important to you. A quiet life in New Hope is important to me."

"You've really thought this through," she mutters.

"Yeah." I swallow hard. "Unfortunately, that's what I do."

She hums softly. "I think I might like your devil's ideas better."

I chuckle and inhale deeply, taking a long hit of her floral shampoo. "You and me both."

* * *

Janelle

I fell asleep in Cade's arms, but when I wake up, I'm in the bed and he's not in the room. I look at the clock, then rub my eyes and look again. It's after nine. I can't believe I slept so late.

I brush my teeth and search my closet for something casual yet sexy but not slutty. I need to walk that careful line where Cade will want to screw my brains out, despite his very logical reasoning against it, but where my brother won't mock me for trying too hard. I decide on tight jeans and a wide-necked T-shirt that falls off one shoulder, and head downstairs.

Nate and Hanna are in the kitchen making fuck-me eyes at each other, and I sneak past and into the den where I hear the television playing.

Cade leans forward, his biceps tensed under his black, fitted T-shirt, his elbows on his denim-clad knees, eyes narrowed as he studies the screen. An old *Roommates* episode is playing, and I grimace to see myself on the screen, my character snapping gum and looking off into the distance like she's not quite bright enough to remember her name most days. I played that role *way* too convincingly.

"Why are you watching this?" I ask, reaching for the remote.

"Shh," Cade says, and grabs the remote from my hand before I can hit the power button. He nods to the screen. "Why didn't you tell me about this?"

I watch the image of myself on the screen flip my hair and roll my eyes and say in total Valley-girl whine, "But he's so *dreamy.*"

"Oh my God." I sink onto the couch beside Cade, and my jaw goes slack as I stare at the screen. "I'd forgotten this episode."

They talked Tom into doing a single episode on the show, and the fans went *crazy* for it. His guest appearance was as a total player who'd been trying to sleep with all three of the female characters without them knowing about his duplicity. His character's thing was to kiss the girls goodnight and whisper, "She loves me. She loves me not." Of course, at the end of the episode, the girls put it together and realize he's trying to get them all in bed and they all dump him at once in a show of friendship and solidarity the show was known for. But Tom was such a heartthrob at the time that even though his character in this episode was a complete slimeball, fans adored even his sleazy line.

Cade shuts off the TV and leans back on the couch, his eyes trained on the dark screen.

"You're not going to convince me this is further evidence against Tom, are you?" I ask. "Clearly, whoever this guy is, he's just obsessed with the show. Maybe he wishes he was Tom."

"Maybe," Cade says. I can't read his expression, but I get the impression he's not ready to share his thoughts with me. He exhales heavily and turns those dark eyes on me. "How'd you sleep?"

"Fantastic. I don't even remember moving to the bed."

"I put you there this morning. Waking up with you in my arms was . . ."

"Nice?" I offer. "The best way to start a day? Amazing?"

The corner of his mouth quirks up in a crooked grin, and he looks toward the doorway, as if to make sure we're still alone. "Tempting."

"Right," I mutter. "Mr. Old-Fashioned."

I don't think he hears me, because he's already heading out of the room. I squeeze my eyes shut and sigh. Last night he opened up and shared so much of himself with me I could hardly keep up, but this morning we're back to one-word reveals. *Maybe* and *tempting*.

The couch shifts as someone sits beside me, and I open my eyes to see Hanna has taken Cade's spot, and she stares at me, studying me like my entire life story is written on my face.

I smile weakly. "Hey, Han. What's up?"

She arches a brow. "When are you going to tell me the real story with the cop? And don't tell me you'd been secretly dating when you kissed Tom. I *know* you, and if you don't tell me the truth soon, I'm going to have an entire explanation in my head and I'm just gonna run with it, whether it's true or not."

I groan. "Can I hear your version first? Then I'll pick the one I like best."

"Okay," she says. "I think he was a cover-up so you didn't lose your contract. But then you two started having feelings for each other. And then your world imploded with psycho daisy guy, and now he's trying to protect you and the feelings are growing with all the bodyguard sexiness, and any minute now Whitney Houston's going to appear from the great beyond and sing 'I Will Always Love You.'"

The last part makes me giggle. I'm not sure if I should be relieved or frightened by how close she is to the truth. I decide to go with relieved and do my best to fill her in. I start at the beginning, grateful to be having this conversation with Hanna and not Nate, because I can tell her details a brother just doesn't need to know.

When I get to the part about our conversation last night, she gives a dreamy sigh and leans her head against my shoulder for a beat.

"I knew he was a good guy, but wow."

I scowl. "I know. Fucking chivalry. Lotta good *that's* doing me."

"He's right, you know," she says.

"I know. Sex will only complicate things, but—"

"No, I mean about Tom. If you're seriously considering getting back together with him . . ." She bites her lip. "Please tell me you're not seriously considering it."

"That's all I thought about while I was trying to sleep last night," I admit. "Well, that is, once I was able to get my filthy, horny mind off Cade's body so close to mine."

"Come up with anything good?" She narrows her eyes. "About Tom, not about Cade's body."

"A week ago, I would have jumped at the chance to be back with Tom." I sigh and roll my eyes. "As evidenced by the tabloid stories about our kiss."

"But now?" Hanna asks.

"Now I'm thinking that if I have a chance with Cade, all I want is for Tom to get out of the way. And if that's true, I shouldn't want to be with Tom at all, should I? I mean, would I have wanted him to stay married to me only because Bella didn't want him? So I start thinking about that more, and I realize . . ." I hesitate, not sure how to say what I'm feeling but still sure that if I can find the words, I'll sound completely pathetic.

"You realized that you don't want Tom back,"

Hanna says. "You just don't want to be alone."

I nod and tears fill my eyes. "Which pretty much tells me what I need to do where Tom's concerned, though it's embarrassing to me that that much wasn't clear from the start."

"I'm proud of you," Hanna says, pulling me into her arms. "Don't feel embarrassed for wanting someone to share your life with. That's a pretty basic human desire. I'm just glad that someone won't be fuckface Tom."

I giggle only because Hanna doesn't typically swear.

"You feel better?" she asks.

I nod. It feels good to have that figured out, even if it doesn't make a difference for Cade. Tom was only one of a litany of reasons he doesn't think we should be involved. We have different lives, and mine is a life he can't stand.

"We're leaving today," Hanna says. "Are you sure you won't come back with us?"

"I'm sure."

She hugs me tighter and whispers, "He's crazy if he thinks he's going to resist you. I'd put money on him caving before the end of the week."

CHAPTER FOURTEEN

Janelle

HANNA WAS SO WRONG. I want to strangle her for giving me false hope.

Cade and I have been cooped up in this house together for ten days.

Ten. Ten awkwardly silent dinners. Ten pervy mornings where I pretended not to stare as Cade returned from his run, sweaty and shirtless. Ten showers where I left the door unlocked or cracked or even wide open, hoping he'd happen by and would, I don't know, actually do some of the dirty shower things he once whispered in my ear. Ten lonely nights in a cold bed. It's all I can do to keep myself from going to him and asking him if I'm misremembering how good it felt when we touched. He can call himself old-fashioned all he wants, but this is the man who gave me the best oral of my life when he didn't even know my name.

Ten days ago, Cade made it clear he was staying

here as my bodyguard and nothing more. He hasn't strayed from that role. Not once. And, not coincidentally, ten days ago my life went from a wild rollercoaster to a serious snoozefest.

The HiLo turned over the footage the police were asking for, and we discovered that we have no idea when Courtney left the bar or through what exit. There are a couple service exits that aren't under video surveillance, but the police have questioned the employees and come up empty. *Super helpful.* Then we found out that the server holding security footage at my condo was hacked from an outside computer, meaning nobody who works in the building was an accessory to Mr. Psycho Rapist. The same day, we learned there was no match in the database for the DNA sample they collected from Courtney's exam, and the florist leads fizzled into nothing.

Six days ago, the networks started playing *Roommates* marathons, the show seeming to get new life from the publicity surrounding "The Daisy Stalker."

Five days ago, I was so desperate for attention from Cade that I pulled on my shortest pair of sleep shorts (I have underwear that covers more) and a tight tank top with no bra and wandered around cleaning the house with a feather duster and lots of bending from the waist. He locked himself in his room with his laptop, and Jamaal laughed at me for a solid hour.

If I'm honest with myself, maybe he's not the only one holding back. I might be leaving the literal door open for him to make his move, but I've kept the figurative door closed by not telling him I have no interest in reuniting with Tom. Maybe I'm afraid he won't believe me. Or maybe I'm scared of Cade rejecting me even after my ex-husband isn't standing between us. I'm not sure my heart could handle that.

Three days ago, Courtney gave a live interview on Ina Turnstall's show, ripping my heart out as she talked about what it's like to wake up every morning with no memory of that night, only the knowledge that someone drugged her and had sex with her without her consent. It was the first time I heard her talk about it. After Cade and I got settled here at Nate's, I called and texted, trying to get together with her. She gave me the runaround every time, and I stopped. I figure she's not up for company—or at least not *my* company—and I didn't want to push it. It was surreal, listening to a woman I used to call my best friend confide more to the whole network audience than she'd been willing to confide in me.

"She's a mess," I told Cade when he walked into the room. He turned on his heel and pulled out his phone, dialing Gormong. From what I could pick up from that conversation, they were not expecting her to do the interview, nor were they happy about it.

Two days ago, Tom called me, demanding to know if Courtney had told me anything about the night she disappeared, wanting to know what I knew about the investigation. The call left me with a bad feeling in my gut, but I decided I shouldn't tell Cade about it. He'd only use it as further evidence that Tom should be a suspect. Tom might be an asshole, but he's no rapist.

Yesterday, I broke down and called my agent for

news on my role as Trista. Helen's still unsure, and the publicity from the case seems to make her even more hesitant to allow me my role. *"She just doesn't want the film to be tainted with all this drama,"* Merriellen said, making me wonder yet again if it will ever feel like she's on my side. And then she started talking about renewed interest in *Roommates*, and an hour later she had a potential movie script couriered to me. *"There are some big players interested. Helen's decision will be irrelevant if this movie happens."*

Ten days, and other than a script for a movie I have very mixed feelings about and Tom's weird phone call, it's been a bunch of nothing. The Daisy Stalker hasn't sent any more letters or flowers. My friends and I have been unharmed, not accounting for harassment from certain members of the press.

Ten days, and I'm losing my flipping mind because Cade treats me like there's a psycho waiting right outside the door, so when my phone rings and it's Courtney asking me to come to her house to hang with her and Jo and their husbands tonight, I am all over it. "We'll be there," I promise without asking Cade.

I call out the plans to Cade through the office door and rush off to take my shower before he can protest. There's nothing he can do to keep me in this house another night. I need to get out.

* * *

HOLDING HER CLOSE

Cade

Oh fuck. I am so screwed.

Janelle walks down the wide marble staircase, and I can't remember how to breathe.

Hands off. That's my plan. Keep my hands off her and my head on straight.

I know I've been testing her patience by keeping her cooped up for the last week and a half, and as much as I wanted to make her stay home tonight, she's just stubborn enough that I fear she'd go without me if I tried. So there she is, dressed in a little black number that hugs every one of her curves and makes my hands itch to roam, explore, touch. *Claim.*

Keeping my distance for the last ten days has tested every inch of my willpower. Knowing she's sleeping a room away, hearing her laugh with Jamaal, watching her curled up with a book and a glass of wine—every second with her makes me want her that much more, but I've had this big house and plenty of space to put between us. Tonight, I won't. At a party with her Hollywood friends, I'll have her by my side and have to pretend to be the loving boyfriend. This will require flirting and touching.

Fuck, am I screwed.

"What?" Janelle asks. She frowns as she looks down at her dress—one of those short, tight, second-skin things that was created with the purpose of making men's heads explode. "After living in my yoga pants lately, I thought it might be fun to dress up a little. Is it okay?"

I swallow hard. "It's perfect." I hold out my hand, encouraging her to come down the remaining steps. That was a rookie mistake, though. Her hand in mine sends electric waves of energy through me. One simple touch and I'm reminded how much I need this woman, how time with her has made that need slingshot past physical into an ache for something more.

Maybe she'd like me to warm her bed until I go home, to fill our nights with slick skin and hot hands and passion better than anything either of us has had before. Maybe I could make her forget that bastard ex of hers, make her realize she deserves so much more. The only thing I know for sure is how much I want to try.

***

Janelle

Cade's silence on the drive is so intense, it's practically ominous. His shoulders are drawn up around his ears and he's practically coiled in on himself, as if he wants to stay as far away from me as possible.

When we get to Courtney's, Davis gives our name at the security gate out front and the guard flips through a couple pages to find our names before waving us through. So much for an intimate dinner. My stomach sinks with disappointment. I hoped tonight might be an opportunity for me to reconnect with my old friends, but it looks like it's just another loud party with a who's-who guest list.

The house is lit up, and music pulses from the backyard. Cade helps me out of the car, his mouth drawn into a tight line. He scans the front of the house, and I can practically hear his brain taking inventory of the half a dozen sports cars lining the circle drive.

"Do you want me to stay?" Davis asks.

Cade nods. "I could use an extra pair of eyes."

I frown at him. "These are friends, not suspects. And anyway, Courtney has her own security on staff tonight. Let Davis have the night off."

The men exchange a look, and Davis nods. For a few days now, after no new developments in the case, I've had to wonder if maybe we've heard the last from our stalker. How long will Cade stay—how long will he put his life on hold waiting for this guy to make his move? But to look at his posture now, the creep might as well be waiting for me behind the nearest bush. I know without them saying that Davis isn't going anywhere.

I shrug. All I care about right now is having a good time tonight. I'm so sick of being stuck in that big house, dwelling on what might or might not happen next, and trying to ignore the way Cade avoids me at all costs.

We head up to the house and are met at the door by Courtney's butler. He leads us to the back of the house where accordion doors are open to the cool night air. The party flows from the massive living room onto the back patio and pool area. At first glance, I can't find Courtney or Jo, but see at least a dozen other people milling around with glasses or wine and bottles of beer.

"What the fuck?" Cade mutters as he scans the crowd for potential rapists and psychos. "I thought it was going to be the two of them and their husbands?"

"Courtney's always been *social*," I explain. "Historically, her small gatherings turn into bigger gatherings. I'm not sure she's capable of arranging an 'intimate' get-together." I smile so he won't see how disappointed I am, how hurt that I'm not part of her inner circle anymore.

Cade lifts his chin. "Let's find her. You can say hi and we can get out of here."

I prop my hands on my hips. "Seriously? What did I do?"

"I'm being cautious, princess."

"You're being unreasonable. *Nothing* has happened. We don't know if anything else *will* happen. I can't stand another day imprisoned in that house, and I want to unwind a little."

Our argument is cut short when someone calls, "Elle!" Courtney bounces across the room to me. "You made it!" She's holding a massive glass of wine and wraps me up in a one-armed hug, rocking back and forth.

I hug her back and squeeze my eyes shut as I breathe her in. "Are you okay?" What a stupid question. Of course she's not okay.

The smile falls off her face, and she shrugs. "I don't want to think about all that tonight. I just want to enjoy some drinks with my close friends."

Cade grunts but doesn't say anything.

"I understand completely." I ignore Cade's decision to channel his inner caveman tonight. It was only a matter of time.

Courtney shifts her focus to Cade, who's poised and ready to tackle all the imaginary bad guys filling the room. "And you're Cade? The boyfriend?"

He offers his hand. "Nice to meet you."

Courtney drags her eyes over him, from head to toe. "Well, aren't you delicious? No wonder she's been keeping you to herself. She doesn't want to share." With a laugh that's as artificial as her double-D cups, she licks her lips. "I wouldn't want to either."

I roll my eyes. "Step off, Court. He's taken." Tonight I'm glad for the lie if it will keep her hands off Cade. Courtney might be married, but that's never stopped her before.

"Elle!" Jo calls behind me. She rushes across the room and nudges Courtney playfully to the side so she can hug me. She, too, has a wine glass, and her cheeks are flushed, as if she's already half tipsy. "I'm so glad you could come!"

"Me too."

The smile falls off my face when I see Bella has followed Jo over, and she waits behind her, a small smirk on her face.

"Hi, Bella." My stomach flips. I didn't know she'd be here, though I guess I should have expected it. "How are you?" Again, a stupid question. And I feel disgusting for asking it. Tom is leaving her because he wants to be with me, and even though I didn't ask him to, it makes me the other woman in our screwed-up dynamic.

"Hi." She looks from Cade to me and back to Cade.

"Oh, God," Courtney says. "I'm sorry. Awkward, huh? Bella is staying with me for a while. But, hey, you two have a lot in common since she kicked Tom's cheating ass to the curb, too. Bella even bought a condo in the same building as Janelle."

"Twinsies," Jo says.

"The difference is that I don't want him back," Bella says. She tops that gem of bitchiness with an eye roll, and I have to tamp down my hatred for her. I would be pissed about the condo thing if I had any intention of going back to mine. But after the break-in, I've already mentally moved out of the place.

"I thought Tom left *you*," Cade says to Bella. "That's the story he's telling."

Bella snorts. "Of course he is, but I ended it. At some point, you've gotta say *enough's enough.*"

"I'm sorry it didn't work out," I say.

"Are you really?" Bella asks. "Or have I done you a favor?"

I blink at her, and I don't manage to find my voice when Courtney says, "Ladies, let's be civil tonight. Bella, focus on the fact that you're about to be free of that philandering pig."

"May he get what's coming to him," Bella says.

Jo lifts her glass taps it against Courtney's. "I'll drink to that."

The ladies drain their glasses in unison and then giggle.

Courtney scans the room. "You two make

yourselves at home. I need to figure out where my waitstaff disappeared to. It's like they expect my guests to get their own drinks."

Jo starts to follow Court, then stops and grabs my arm. "Hey, did you read the script?"

I nod. "It felt like being sucked into a time warp."

Courtney skids to a stop at the mention of the script. "I know, right?"

Jo laughs. "I'm practically giddy."

"There isn't even an offer on the table yet," I remind her. "Don't get too excited yet."

"What do you think?" Courtney asks. "I wasn't sure I was interested, but if Kopperman gets involved, you know we'll get a big budget."

"You weren't sure you were interested?" Bella mutters. "You've practically been salivating since your agent called."

"I'd forgotten how much those characters make me laugh," I admit. And since it looks like my opportunity to play Trista has been lost, I know I'll take this role if anyone remotely credible offers the opportunity. The only thing worse than being a pigeonholed actress is being an unemployed actress. It's been too long since I've had a job more meaningful than a shampoo commercial.

Courtney shakes her head. "It's insane, you know. When *Roommates* wrapped up, I wouldn't have thought I'd be excited about this, but now it's like I can't wait to get back to it."

I can't help but notice Bella hanging back, looking a little left out. I know what that's like. I've been the odd man out since she befriended Court and Jo. Then again, with those two, maybe I always was.

Courtney points to her empty glass. "Anyway, I seriously need to do something about this. Let's talk more later."

"Bella," I call, before she can follow the girls.

"Yeah?" She sets her jaw and folds her arms in a defensive stance.

"I wanted you to know I'm not going back to Tom. Not even when the divorce is final." I grimace. I feel like I've been eating a lot of crow lately, but just because Bella's a bitch doesn't mean I don't owe her an apology. "I'm truly sorry about everything, but I'm glad you're standing up for yourself. You deserve better."

She blinks at me, her eyes widening and her mouth falling open. "Thanks." She smirks at Cade before looking back to me. "I can see why Tom won't be getting you back. Way to trade up."

When she walks away, I can feel Cade's eyes on me.

He draws in a breath and stares at me for a long beat. "Dance with me." It's not a question, and he doesn't wait for a response. He leads me to the patio where several other couples are dancing and takes me into his arms.

My eyes float closed at the power his presence has over me, how good it feels to be in his arms, how safe I feel when he's holding me this close.

Damn. He smells incredible.

"Do you wear cologne?" I ask.

"Why?"

"Because you smell so good, I'm thinking of

funding a national campaign to have every man wear what you do." I sigh. "Then again, that might mean I'd get turned on every time I breathed through my nose, which could be problematic."

His lips twitch into a lopsided grin. "I've never been much of a cologne man. You're probably smelling my aftershave." His gaze drops to my lips and stays there, and my heart flutters in a syncopated rhythm four out of five doctors would probably call a cause for concern.

"I like it."

"You smell good too," he murmurs.

"Yeah? Because the way you've been avoiding me, I thought maybe I had body odor and didn't know it."

He chuckles and pulls me tighter against him until my head rests on his shoulder, and I can't see his face anymore. "I'm keeping my distance because I can't trust myself when I'm close to you. When you're close, I want to get you naked."

Uh-oh. There goes my heart again. "That's bad?"

"I thought it was, but now I can't decide. On the one hand, everything's too complicated, and sex isn't known for uncomplicating anything. There's the investigation." He swallows. "There's the fact that we live in different worlds."

I could say that none of that matters, but we both know it's a lie. The truth is, that's all been on my mind too. Do I want to push Cade into a physical relationship with me if doing so only sets me up for heartbreak? "I thought you liked complications."

He pulls back to look at my face and tucks a lock of hair behind my ear. "I don't want someone I care about to be hurt by them."

My stomach dances in acrobatic leaps to the unsteady beat of my heart.

"One second," he says, "I'm determined to stay away from you. To keep my hands off you so I can keep my head clear."

"And the next second?" I ask.

"The next second I'm thinking about making you moan and feeling you come when I'm inside you."

I lean my head on his shoulder and try to remember how to breathe. "I've missed your dirty mouth."

He dips his head and his lips brush my ear as he says, "And I've missed the things my dirty mouth does to you."

CHAPTER FIFTEEN

Cade

I CAN HARDLY THINK WHEN SHE'S this close to me. Smelling so damn good and tempting me so damn much. With each breath of her, a million images flash through my mind. Janelle under me and screaming my name; Janelle in the shower, her fist wrapped around my dick as she drops to her knees; Janelle riding me as I tease her nipples. I want to taste every inch of her, to discover how many times I can make her come in one night.

"How long are you going to protect me?" Her voice cracks on the question, and before I can answer—or even mentally catch up—she asks the next. "What if they don't find the guy next week or the week after? How long are you going to put your life on hold?"

She's not the only one who's asked this. Gormong asks daily, and my boss in New Hope is getting impatient. "As long as it takes."

"I think you've more than made amends for any

karmic debt the thing with Cara made you feel." She releases a humorless chuckle. "Don't get me wrong. I want you here—right now, tomorrow morning, next week. But I know how selfish I'm being by keeping you in a town you hate."

"Don't do that." I brush my knuckles across her cheek. "I came here because of my guilt over what happened with Cara, but this isn't about that anymore. It hasn't been for a long time. It's about *you*." I pause for a moment, mentally calculating how much longer we need to stay at this damn party with its too-fucking-many people. "Talk to me."

"About what?"

I shrug. "Tell me about the script the girls were asking about."

She hesitates for a minute, as if she's not sure why I want to know, then she seems to understand I'm trying to distract us both. We both lose our minds when we touch. "It's a film about the girls from *Roommates*. It's part romantic comedy, part reunion movie. They tossed around the idea after the show was canceled but no one was really interested. We'd run our course. But now everyone suddenly cares about us again. At least it would be something positive to come out of all this."

"You'd do it?" I brush my knuckles over her bare shoulder, just for the chance to feel her skin. "I thought you wanted to do something different with your career."

She tenses, and even though she's still in my arms, she physically withdraws. "I do, but Helen isn't coming around. Trista wasn't just the role of a lifetime; it was the only work of any substance I've had in years. A *Roommates* movie might be silly, but it'd be something to get me noticed again. It could save my dying career." She blows out a breath. "I'm sorry. You didn't deserve any of that rant."

"Don't worry about it." I press a kiss to the top of her head and settle my hand at her waist. I don't want any animosity between us tonight, and asking about her career was a bad call on my part. "That makes sense. Tell me about Courtney and Jo. How long have you three been friends?"

She looks out across the backyard, where dozens of guests mill around, drinking and talking, some dancing. "We didn't meet until we were cast in *Roommates*. As you would expect, we ended up spending a lot of time together on and off set. I've always been close to my brother and his friends but had a hard time making girl friends. Courtney and Jo were tight from the beginning. It was as if they spent every waking moment together. But they included me a lot, and it was nice. We had a lot of fun."

And yet that's not the dynamic I saw inside. Courtney and Jo as besties? Sure. But there was distance between the two of them and Janelle. "When did that change?"

"That obvious, huh?" She swallows hard. "After I caught my husband cheating on me with Bella, I couldn't trust anyone. He really changed me. Even Courtney and Jo . . . I don't know. I like to blame the end of our friendship on Bella swooping in to make them her friends, but the truth is, I didn't trust them. I always felt like they talked about me when I wasn't around, like they wouldn't hesitate to stab me in the back if it served them. And I suddenly started feeling like my entire relationship with these women I'd called my best friends was completely shallow. I need to take some responsibility for that. I know I can be cold and hard to connect to." She drops her gaze to my chest. "Trust me, Tom made *sure* I knew that when our marriage was ending."

I tip her face up until she looks at me. "I don't think you're cold at all. Even when you were dressed in patent leather and a mask and wouldn't tell me your name, I felt an instant connection with you."

Her tensed shoulders drop. "I knew I liked you for a reason."

"I like you too, princess. Tell me it's true. That you're not going back to Tom." Maybe I should try to hide some of the hope in my voice, but I can't.

She chews on the corner of her mouth and shakes her head. "I'm not. I don't want Tom."

I've been waiting for those words, and I feel like this is the first full breath I've taken since he showed up at our hotel room. "Have you talked to him?" Something made her change her mind, and I want to know what. "I mean, since the day at the hotel?"

* * *

Janelle

Have I talked to Tom?

I swallow hard. I don't want to lie to Cade, but I don't like the way my conversation with Tom will implicate him in the investigation when they need to be focused on actual bad guys. I skirt the question altogether. "It wasn't anything Tom said. I just want better. I realized . . ." I study him and swallow hard. I know I owe my realization to Cade and the way his attention and affection make me feel, but I don't want to reveal too much about his role in my decision. I'm afraid he'll think I expect more from him than he's willing to give. "I realized I was only considering it because I was lonely and maybe a little sentimental. But I don't want to be with him, and I realized even giving it a chance would be three steps back for me."

"Thank God," he murmurs against my hair.

We dance in silence, our bodies pressed together as we sway to the loud music. I'm faintly aware of the crowd around us—the splashing in the pool, the laughter of Courtney's guests. I thought this was where I wanted to be tonight. I thought I wanted the distraction of friends and booze, but that's all a shallow substitute for what I really wanted—Cade's attention, his touch. Now that I have it, I don't want to be here at all. I don't know how much longer I get Cade, and I don't want to share that time with anyone, especially not former friends whom I don't even feel a bond with anymore.

When the song ends, I step out of his arms. "Can we

leave?"

Cade nods and leads me to the door without question. I should say my goodbyes, thank the hostess and all that, but she probably won't even notice I'm gone.

Davis is waiting out front with the car. After I climb into the backseat with Cade, I pull out my phone and tap in a quick thank-you text to Courtney. When I look up, Cade is pressing the button to raise the privacy screen.

My mind immediately circles back to the last time we shared the backseat of this car with that screen up. How it felt to be on my knees before him, the feel of his hand in my hair as I pulled him deep into my mouth.

When Davis starts the car, Cade says, "I promised myself I wouldn't touch you tonight."

"Because it's complicated?"

"Complicated as fuck," he whispers, "and getting more so by the day."

Unsure what to say, I look at the passing lights along the highway outside the window. I've made it clear what I want, and I'm not going to throw myself at him—or at least I'm going to try not to. *Dear God, please don't let me throw myself at him. Save me from begging this man for more than he's willing to give.*

I know he wants me, and I could probably persuade him, but I don't want to *persuade* Cade to make love to me. If we do this, there will be complications. One or both of us is going to end up hurt. I want Cade to want me enough that he believes one night together might just be worth the resulting casualties.

"Come here." He grabs my hand and tugs me toward his lap.

Straddling him, I look into his eyes. "The windows are up," I remind him. "There are no cameras. No one is watching."

"Good," he says. "Because what I want to do to you is only about us. You and me and fucking feeling good. It's not about your ex, or your producer, or the sick fuck who's after you." He strokes his thumb along the edge of my jaw before tracing my bottom lip. "It's about you and how amazing you are. How different you are than any woman I've been with before."

I stare into his eyes, looking for the words he didn't say. *Any woman I've* loved *before*. He didn't say that, but I want to believe it's there—that he's fallen for me as completely as I've fallen for him.

"I'm—" I shake my head. "Cade, there's nothing amazing about me. I'm just a washed-up actress with a laundry list of mistakes."

"You're better than every single person in that party. Present company included."

He had me before, but with these words, he's taken my heart into his hands, and I know he can break me.

I lean forward and press my mouth to his, drinking him in with small sips. He draws my bottom lip between his teeth and sucks. Our mouths open and our tongues slide together as his hands cup my ass.

He tears his mouth from mine. "I need you alone."

"It wouldn't be the first time we've messed around back here."

"You think I need you to remind me?" He presses a

kiss to the edge of my jaw. I start to back away, to drop to the floor again, but he holds me still. "I don't need you to remind me how you looked on your knees with my cock in your mouth."

"Are you sure?" I ask.

"The image is burned on my brain. It's my favorite thing to think about when I have my dick in my hand and am fighting the urge to come to your room."

"Don't fight it," I whisper. "I lie in bed thinking about the same thing."

His nostrils flare and his gaze drops to my mouth. "You fantasize about sucking me off?"

Licking my lips, I shrug. "Do you fantasize about going down on me?"

"Fuck yes. At least a dozen times an hour."

The car goes silent until I can't hold back my question anymore. "What's going to happen when we get back to the house?" I hesitate then press forward. "Are we going to do this?"

"Are you asking if I'm going to fuck you?"

My breath catches. "Yeah."

He kisses me softly and slides a hand into my hair. "I don't think that's the question anymore."

"Then what is?"

"Am I going to fuck you before or after I bury my face in your pussy?"

The car stops, right on cue, and Cade and I climb out in charged silence.

He keeps his hand on my arm as we race in the front door and are greeted by Jamaal in the foyer.

Cade gives him a nod of acknowledgment and leads

me toward the stairs and straight to the bedroom, locking the door behind us.

"Finally," he breathes, stepping back and raking his gaze over me.

I unzip my dress and let it fall to the floor. When I step out of it, Cade's lips part, and he seems to stop breathing. His eyes roam over every inch of me, from my black thigh-highs to my lace thong up to my matching bra.

As an actress, physical beauty is a prerequisite, and of all my insecurities, this isn't one. But with Cade, it's never been as simple as feeling beautiful. Beauty is cheap, and in this town it's everywhere you look. Cade looks at me like my beauty is special. As if it's something that can't be found anywhere else.

I reach for the clips holding my thigh-high stockings to my garter belt.

"Leave them," he says, his voice rough. "Those . . . *fuck*. I thought it was hard to keep my hands off you in that dress, but if I had any idea what you were wearing beneath it, I don't think we would have made it out the door tonight."

I bite back a smile as I saunter toward him. I like seeing him like this—pupils dilated, nostrils flared, hands fisted at his sides as if he's clinging to the edge of control. I push him backward into the bedroom's sitting area and until the backs of his legs hit the chair. When I give his chest a light shove, he collapses into it. His eyes are trained on me like I'm a goddess and he's grateful for the opportunity to worship.

He wraps his hands around my legs, stroking the

backs of my thighs with his fingertips before pulling me onto his lap. "Could you be more perfect?"

I shake my head. I want him to see me—the real me. "I'm not perfect. I've done things I'm not proud of."

"Like what?"

My gut flips at the idea of admitting my lowest moment. "Not tonight, okay? I don't want to bring those decisions in this room. I just want you to know I'm not perfect. I sold my soul for my career a long time ago. Don't convince yourself I'm someone I'm not."

He shakes his head and kisses the corner of my mouth. "You're still in total possession of your soul, Janelle Crane. I know because I see it when I look into your eyes."

"All I've ever had was my career." I graze my fingertips along his jaw, relishing the feel of his stubble. "When you only have one thing, you do whatever it takes to cling to it. I'm still an actress. I'm still the woman who hired a man to fix her reputation. I'm the woman who knows hiring Matt isn't the worst she's done. Is that who you want?"

"I know who you are, and I know what I want. I want you more than I've ever wanted anyone." As if to prove his point, he lifts his hips, the thick length of his erection a delicious pressure between my legs.

"Watching you leave is going to be hard enough," I admit. "If we do this, letting you walk away is only going to be harder." I squeeze my eyes shut and will him to tell me that he won't be walking away, that he won't be leaving.

He tucks a lock of hair behind my ear and brushes his lips along my jaw. "I know. Maybe that's part of what made me hold back," he says. "But I've known for a while now that regardless of whether or not we sleep together, I'm going to be a fucking wreck when this ends." He holds me close and skims his lips down the column of my neck until my breath catches. "Maybe when it's over, I want you to be just as fucked up by it as I am."

"Already done," I whisper, and I tell my heart it's not allowed to break. Not yet. Not until it's over.

He skims his knuckles over the lace of my thigh-highs. "I don't want to forget you like this. You're the sexiest thing I've ever seen. Never in my life have I wanted anything as much as I want you."

The thrill at his words races up my spine and tugs on my heart. "I've been wearing my sexiest underwear every single day we've been here together, hoping you might see it. You like it?"

"I love it. You're beautiful. So fucking beautiful." He shakes his head. "That word's not enough."

I press a finger to his lips. "You make me feel better than beautiful. Even when you're avoiding me." I roll my hips, and my eyes float shut as I feel the length of his erection between my legs. "I've never felt like this. Never wanted a man the way I want you." My fingers shake at the buttons of his shirt.

He takes a fistful of my hair and drags my mouth down to meet his in a kiss that matches my hunger.

I pull open the end table drawer and retrieve a condom. "I've had ten days to stash them everywhere,"

I say to his questioning look. "Just in case."

"Hell," he breathes. His eyes skim over me, devouring every inch. "Let me touch you first. We don't have to—"

"Two weeks of foreplay might push my limits." I tear it open before lifting to drag his pants down his hips and rolling the condom down his shaft. "This is what I need right now."

Returning to straddle him, I settle my knees on either side of his hips. There isn't much to these panties, so I have to do little more than pull them to the side before lowering myself onto him.

He swallows hard but keeps his eyes locked on mine as I slowly take him deep. He's thick, and my body aches as I stretch around him, but then I move again and it's so good.

"Christ," he groans.

I use my legs to shift over him, working my way up and down his length and releasing a little gasp every time he's deep. Cade's eyes stay locked on mine, and I have to fight to keep mine open, to keep my head when I want to surrender to the pleasure. One hand grips my hip, firm and demanding. The other cups my breast and teases the nipple through the lace, gentle and promising.

I link my arms behind his neck and lose myself in his murmurs. *"You're gorgeous . . . Just like that . . . Christ, you feel so good."*

When I think I can't stand another second, Cade changes the angle of his hips, shifting to the edge of the chair and driving deeper. I cry out, so full of him and pleasure and need that I want him to stop and give me more all at once. He reaches between our bodies to stroke me.

I squeeze around him, my orgasm coming in a ripple of sensation that seems to stretch from my chest through my legs and roll out like waves, and just when I think every inch of release has been wrung from my body, he finds his own, and the swell of him inside me sets off a new wave of pleasure as I follow him down.

After, the room seems so bright and so silent that I'm not sure I can hide the emotion filling every inch of me, and I'm afraid if he sees it, he'll pull away.

I bury my face in his neck and squeeze my eyes shut.

"What's wrong?" he whispers.

I shake my head, and he pulls away from me until I'm forced to look at him. Can he see it in my eyes? He's so afraid of hurting me, and I can't let him know the truth. He's already hurting me because he's planning to walk away—not just from LA, but from me and this world he hates, this world that is part of who I am, part of what I want for my life. I've handed over my heart, and when he leaves, it will break. I know this, and I know I would suffer fracture after fracture for these moments in his arms.

"Tell me," he says.

"It's just . . . a lot," I say. "I'm a little overwhelmed."

Cupping my jaw in his palms, he presses his mouth to mine and kisses me with long, greedy strokes of his tongue. "Me too," he whispers against my mouth. "It's been a long time since I've felt anything like this."

He takes me to the bed, and I use my hands and

body to say all the things I'm afraid to say with words.

CHAPTER SIXTEEN

Cade

I WAKE UP TO THE SOUND of my phone ringing, and it takes me a minute to orient myself. Where I am? There's a pillow under my head, a fan humming above me, sheets tangled around my legs, and Janelle—naked in my arms.

Right. *Heaven.* I'm in heaven.

I carefully extricate myself and climb out of bed to grab my cell. This time of night, it can't be good. When I see the caller ID and see Gormong's name, I know it's not.

"What happened?" I ask.

"Jo O'Connor. She disappeared from a party at Courtney's tonight. I can't talk long, but I thought you'd want to know."

"Right." *Fuck. Shit.* I knew having all those people at that party was trouble waiting to happen, and now my gut's crawling into my throat and a thousand what-ifs are invading my brain. *What if Janelle had gone without me? What if it had been her?* "Thanks for calling."

"Janelle's accounted for?"

I know she's behind me, but I turn anyway, needing to reassure myself that she's here and safe. She's sitting up, the sheet gripped in her fist between her breasts. The fear in her eyes tightens something in my chest. "She's with me."

"Keep her close," Gormong says. "Our IT guys are close to a break. If you can just keep her safe for a few more days . . ."

"Call when you know more," I say. With every second I'm on the phone, the panic on Janelle's face rises. "I'll tell Janelle."

I end the call, but she's already out of bed and pulling on a robe. "Courtney or Jo?" She shivers and rubs her arms.

"Jo," I say softly. "She disappeared from the party."

She blinks and swallows hard. "So while we were . . .?" She waves a hand and shivers again. "She was . . .? How did no one see him? How did no one see her leave? How did he even get in?"

I draw her against me. I don't have any answers, and any reassurances I could offer will ring hollow in light of what we know about Courtney's abduction.

"She must be so scared right now. What does he want from us?" Her shivers grow harsh and persistent. Seeing her like this cuts at something inside me.

I scoop her into my arms and carry her over to the bed. Pulling back the covers, I lower her onto the mattress and climb in behind her. Inside our cocoon of blankets, I wrap my arms around her.

She seems so small and the tremors racking her body seem so big.

"I've got you," I whisper, smoothing her hair back. "I'm here and you're safe. I promise. I won't let anything happen to you. Breathe for me, beautiful." I wipe the tears from her cheeks and she does as I ask, taking a slow inhale and then releasing the air. "Now close your eyes. I'm right here."

She obeys, and her breathing slows. I wonder if she's fallen asleep when she speaks again. The words come out on a ragged exhale. "I'm scared."

I pull her against me so we're skin to skin. "Hold on to that. Fear isn't always bad. Sometimes it keeps you safe."

* * *

I hate leaving her. Until we catch this guy, having her anywhere but by my side makes me antsy as hell, but Gormong asked me to come to the station first thing this morning. I left the house as soon as I knew both Davis and Jamaal were alert and debriefed on what happened. Jo's disappearance has already been leaked to the press, so the end of Nate's drive is crowded with reporters.

"We picked up the hacker this morning," Gormong says as he leads me into the conference room. "But he's not talking yet."

"Does he know where Jo is?"

"No, and he has an alibi for all night last night. We believe someone hired him. He'll tell us who if he doesn't want to face time for rape and abduction." He waves to the chairs facing a large projection screen. "Take a seat. I need to show you something."

"What is it?"

Gormong nods toward the screen. He hits a button on the remote and the image of a mansion fills the screen. Not just any mansion—Courtney's place. "Courtney's security staff handed over their surveillance footage this morning. They have cameras around the perimeter of the house."

"You got him on camera?"

"I don't know," he says, as a blonde saunters on screen. "That's Jo." Pointing the remote at the screen, he fast-forwards, and I watch the time stamp tick through nearly three hours of Jo on- and off-screen, dancing, drinking, and talking with dozens of different people. Throughout the night, her walk turns to a stagger. She's drunk. Or is she drugged? Both?

Gormong hits a different button and the scene changes to the view of the front of the house. This must be a different camera, and the timestamp is ten minutes later. "Watch on the left," he says.

She leans against the side of the house, just barely in the frame. Her face is half in shadow, but there's enough light to make out her surprise as a man comes onto the screen, presses her against the building, and kisses her. Gormong hits pause, and I tilt my head as I study the image.

"Is that who I think it is?" I ask.

"I don't know," Gormong says, his voice low. "But if you're thinking it looks an awful lot like Tom Comer, you're not alone."

* * *

Janelle

"Tom! What a surprise."

"Sorry I didn't call." Tom drags a hand through his hair and shakes his head. "I was afraid you'd tell me not to come."

"Good guess," Jamaal says from beside me. "Why don't you follow that instinct and excuse yourself?"

I shoot Jamaal a glare. Tom's obviously upset about Jo's disappearance—as he should be. Jo spent a lot of time with us when Tom and I were married. Hell, Tom and Jo would sometimes even go out without me. They're good friends. Jamaal could at least be empathetic. Everyone's a bit of a mess right now. "Can Tom and I talk in private for a minute?"

When the guard at the front of the drive told me Tom was here to see me, I wasn't sure what to think, but I told him to send him on through. I figure Tom's just as freaked out as the rest of us. And besides, we're overdue for a conversation.

Jamaal scowls at Tom, and I scowl at Jamaal. I'm just as stubborn as he is, and I'm going to win this one.

"We'll be right out back by the pool. *Relax.*"

Jamaal grumbles something about spoiled divas not knowing what's good for them. I ignore him and lead Tom to the back.

He tucks his hands in his pockets then removes them to adjust his shirt, then his hair. He can't stop fidgeting, and the dark circles under his eyes tell me he had as much trouble sleeping last night as I did.

"I'm freaking out," he says.

"About Jo?" I ask. "I think we're all freaking out. I'd be worried if we weren't."

He squeezes his eyes shut, then opens them and looks at me. "I've made a lot of mistakes, but I'm ready to change. I want to change for you." He reaches for me and grips my shoulders. "Let's leave. Remember when we'd talk about leaving this country and buying a place in Haiti? Let's do it. Let's go. I don't want to be the man I used to be. Not anymore. Leave with me."

Frowning, I shake my head. "No. I can't just . . ."

"Yes, you can. You said you missed me. Let's be together again, and let's start now."

"I'm not going to be with you at all, Tom." I step away from his touch. Once, there was nothing more comforting than his hands on me. Not anymore. "Not now and not ever."

He drops his hands and his face falls. "But I thought . . ."

"You're the first man I ever loved," I say softly. "But it's time for me to let that go."

"The first?" he asks. "What we have is more than that."

I hold his gaze. In the not-physically-abusive division, Tom Comer is a contender for World's Worst Husband, and he's consistently a self-centered asshole. But I loved him once. In his own screwed-up way, I know he still loves me, and that's enough to make me want to proceed cautiously.

"I'm the only man you've ever loved. That means something."

"But it's not true."

His Adam's apple bobs as he swallows. "You're in love with him," he says. "Jesus. I thought it was just for the press, but you fell for the cop."

"I'm sorry."

He looks away and stares at the pool. "Sorry that you love him, or that you can't be with me?"

"I'm sorry I hurt you. When you divorced me, I told myself maybe it wasn't over. Maybe you'd come back to me. That was a mistake."

"It wasn't." He doesn't look hopeful. He looks desperate. "You were right. We're good together."

I wait for these words to wrap me up in their spell. They don't. Tom always had this power to make me forget all reason, but that's gone now. "We're not. We loved each other, but we weren't good together. Waiting for you was a mistake because it kept me from moving on."

"I need you now, Elle. I know you don't believe me, but let me prove it." He turns away, shaking his head and studying the concrete. "I left my wife for you. If I would have known . . ."

Still a liar, even in the same breath that he swears he

wants to change. But I don't mention that Bella said she kicked him out. It's not relevant. "If you were willing to leave her for me, you shouldn't have been with her at all. She deserves better than that."

He grunts. "If you believe that, you don't know Bella very well. That woman is pure evil."

Shrugging, I rock onto my toes and press a kiss to his cheek. "This is goodbye."

With a final grimace, he nods and squeezes my hands in his. "I have to leave town. If you need anything, you can call my lawyer, but I've gotta get out of here."

My gut turns cold. "Tom, what's going on?"

He doesn't answer, and for the first time I notice how bloodshot his eyes are. This isn't just worry and lack of sleep.

"Why did you call me after Courtney was on TV?" I ask, and he winces. "You wanted to know what she said to me. And now Jo's gone and you're freaked out again. Why, Tom? What's going on?"

"I can't talk about this," he says.

"Why not?" I ask.

"Because he doesn't want to tell you the truth." Cade's at the back door, his arms crossed, his face hard.

Tom follows my gaze and winces. "Listen—"

"Officer Gormong," Cade calls, and the officer steps onto the patio and toward Tom.

"We need to ask you a few questions," Gormong says to Tom.

Tom takes a step back, then he turns his gaze on me. "I didn't do anything. Whatever happens in the next few days, I want you to know I didn't do anything wrong."

I turn from Cade to Tom, and I can't get my footing. "I don't understand. Someone explain this."

Cade stands frozen, watching Tom leave.

"What's happening?"

"I could ask you the same thing," he says, his voice cold. His whole body is cold. He's shut himself off from me again, as if all he has to do is flip a switch.

"He came here asking for me to leave town with him, to start over." I frown in the direction Tom and Gormong disappeared. "What's going on?"

"I can't tell you."

"What? Sure you can." I fold my arms. "I told him I didn't want to be with him. Why are you acting like a dick all of a sudden?"

He releases a dry laugh. "Your ex-husband called you about the case and you didn't even tell me. I asked if you'd talked to him, and you lied to me to protect him. What can I say? That brings out my dickish side."

"I didn't lie. I didn't want you to know about that conversation because I thought you'd think . . ." *Exactly what any good cop would think.*

Oh my God, Tom. What have you done?

"You deliberately kept the truth from me."

It seemed harmless at the time, but Cade has gone so cold I wish I could take it back. "You don't really think he's capable of this, do you?"

"We're a simple DNA test away from proving he drugged and raped your best friends, and I find out he's here. With you. But hey, at least it wasn't against your will. Small blessings, right?"

"A DNA test?" That was why Tom was so freaked out. He knew they were coming for him. And the only reason he would know they were coming for him is if he did it. "No. Cade." I shake my head. "You have to stop Gormong. You don't understand. Tom wouldn't ever—"

"We'll talk about this later. I need to go into the station. They found Jo at her house." Any relief I feel at those words is lost when he sneers. "She doesn't have any memory of what happened last night, and she's a mess. Maybe you should worry about her more than you worry about Tom. Stay in the house. Don't talk to the press."

* * *

Cade

When I get to the station, Gormong already has Tom in an interview room. "You question him yet?" I ask as I watch Tom through the one-way glass.

One second, I was watching Tom on the surveillance video. The next, the security guy who works the gate at Nate's was calling me to let me know Janelle had just let Tom back to the house.

It might take a month for my heart rate to return to normal.

"I was letting him sweat for a while first," Gormong

says. "Want to join me?"

"After you," I say, motioning to the door.

Tom's expression is cold when we walk into the room, and he keeps his arms crossed.

Gormong doesn't say a word, and opts for the strong visual instead. He grabs the remote off the table, presses play, and lets the surveillance footage from last night speak for itself.

As Tom watches it, the color drains from his face.

"Do you want to explain that?" Gormong says, taking a seat across from him.

I stay standing and study Tom, trying to decipher what kind of guilt I'm seeing on his face. The guilt of a major criminal or the guilt of a married man whose affair has just been exposed?

"Christ, they're evil," he finally mutters.

"What do you mean by that?" Gormong asks.

Tom looks to me. "You of all people know how heartless actresses can be."

My jaw tightens, but I don't respond. If this fucker thinks I'm on his side, he's got another thing coming.

"What happened last night?" Gormong asks. "We know you went to the party. Leaving your name on guest register at the front gate was pretty fucking sloppy."

"Why wouldn't I sign in? I was invited. I didn't do anything wrong."

Gormong shoots me a look and sighs. "Let's talk about it. You see her at the party, get a little frisky. Does a fancy actor like you have to drug his women to get laid?"

"She fucking *called* me," Tom says. "She begged me to come."

"Sure," Gormong said. "But if she begged you, why drug her? Why abduct her or tie her up? I'm guessing her rape kit will show the same thing Courtney's did. And when we test that semen against your DNA . . ."

He snaps back in his chair as if Gormong smacked him. "You think *I'm* the kidnapper? Why the fuck would I kidnap and rape a couple of women I can hardly keep off my dick?"

Gormong's jaw ticks. "What's that supposed to mean?"

"They . . . we . . . ." Tom looks to either side, as if trying to find a friendly face. "We have a history, okay? Sometimes those girls will be out, and they'll get worked up. They know I'm good for it." He drags a hand over his face. "But for Christ's sake, I didn't take either of them anywhere those nights but back home after we fucked in the back of my limo."

"You admit to having sex with them?" Gormong asks.

"Yeah, but sex isn't rape when they beg you for it."

Part of me is shocked that he's admitting to it. Another part of me knows that guys like Tom believe they can get away with anything.

"Courtney's last memory is of being in the club," Gormong says. "You picked her up and fucked and say you *took her home*?"

"Yes!" Tom says. "I swear."

"Jo's last memory is of being at Courtney's," Gormong continues. "You're telling me you did the same thing? Picked her up, fucked her, and took her home?"

"That's all. I don't know what happened after I took them home, but that's all that happened."

Gormong folds his arms. "You were with both women the nights they disappeared but you never mentioned this to anyone? Don't you think that's important?"

Tom's gaze darts to mine and his cheeks redden. "I'm a married man."

I choose that moment to end my silence. "I thought you were working on divorce papers."

Tom and Gormong turn to me at the same time. Tom says, "I didn't want Janelle to know either. That's not exactly a solid ground for reconciliation."

"Or you're a sick fuck who's been stalking these women for weeks and screwing with their minds." I lean over the table. There's too much anger pumping through my system, and when I feel Gormong's hand on my arm, I know I need to tread carefully. "You didn't think you'd be caught."

"Fuck this." Tom slams his palms against the table. "I'm being set up. Courtney called me from the HiLo that night. I assumed our hookup was completely unrelated to her disappearance, but then when Jo disappeared after we hooked up last night . . ." He shakes his head. "They're setting me up. The 'Loves me not' thing? That's from the time I was on *Roommates*. My character was trying to sleep with all three girls, and Court and Jo thought it was hilarious because . . ." His gaze snaps up to meet mine.

"Because you were sleeping with all three of them in real life," I fill in. "While you were married to Janelle, you were fucking her two best friends."

"I like women, okay? But I'm not a fucking rapist. They're setting me up," he says. "They get fame again. They get their fucking movie. And I get *fucked*. You have to believe me. I didn't rape anyone. They called and I came."

"And what about the hacker?" Gormong asks. "We have a paper trail proving you hired him to cover your tracks after you broke into Janelle's condo?" He's good. To study his face, you'd never know he was bluffing. We don't know who hired the hacker. "Do you have an explanation for that too?"

"What hacker?" Tom asks.

"You want to keep playing dumb with me, boy?" Gormong asks. "How's that working out for you so far?"

Tom's face hardens. "I want my lawyer."

"Fine," Gormong says. He turns to me. "Let's give the man his phone call. Guilty men need lawyers."

I follow Gormong out of the interview room and down the hall to his office where he kicks the wall.

"Motherfucker," he says.

"What's wrong?"

He lifts his eyes to mine and studies me for a beat. "I don't want to, Cade, I swear."

"Don't want to what?"

"I don't want to believe the son-of-a-bitch. But I do."

CHAPTER SEVENTEEN

Janelle

I'M WAITING ON THE COUCH when Cade returns to the house. He walks in the door and treads heavily into the living room before dropping his keys. His shoulders are tensed up like he's carrying the weight of the world there. Or at least the weight of the investigation.

After he left, I took a long, hot shower, and had a good cry. I can't wrap my mind around Tom being responsible for the horrible things Courtney and Jo have been through.

Tom's vain, prideful, and selfish, and under those shining qualities is a deeply insecure man whom, time and again, I've seen hurt others to bolster his own confidence.

But stalking and rape? That doesn't make sense. None of this does.

Cade takes a seat. He's next to me but he doesn't look at me or touch me. He might as well be a hundred miles away.

There are too many things I want to say. I don't know where to start.

I screwed up. . . I'm sorry. . . Let's get through this together. . .

I love you.

Cade's the first to break the silence. "Should I pack my things?"

"What? No." When he finally looks at me, I see pain in his eyes. "I don't want you to leave," I whisper. "I want you to forgive me."

"Fuck." He pulls me into his arms, and those invisible miles between us dissolve the instant I rest my cheek against his chest. I want to cling to him, but I don't let myself.

"I shouldn't have kept his call from you, and I'm sorry. I still can't let myself imagine he might be guilty, but I knew the call would be important to you, so I should have shared it."

He squeezes me tight and I can hear him swallow hard. "I just want to keep you safe."

There are too many words in that sentence. Why can't he just want to *keep* me? Be with me? "I know."

"Can you promise me something?" he asks. "If the evidence proves that Tom is guilty, don't do anything stupid to try to protect him. As it is, he's gotten more from you than he deserves."

I pull back so I can study his face. His features have softened and his eyes have worry lines all around them. "What do you know that you aren't you telling me?"

He shakes his head. "I can't say yet. I'm sorry. I want to tell you more, but . . ."

"It's okay. I understand." All night, I've gotten a sick feeling in my gut every time I think about Tom's call and how freaked out he was after Courtney's interview. Now that sick feeling has grown to fill my whole abdomen. "If Tom is guilty, that's just something I'll have to come to terms with."

He kisses me hard, his hands wrapped around my shoulders.

"Let me cook you dinner," I say when he releases me. "I know the best recipe for twice-baked potatoes. Maybe with a steak?"

"I didn't know you cooked." The corner of his mouth hitches up into a crooked grin.

I climb off the couch and shoot him a grin over my shoulder, trying to lighten the mood. "There's a lot you don't know about me."

The grin falls away and he swallows hard. "I know."

* * *

Cade

This shitty day ended with a pretty fantastic night.

We had dinner and wine on the back patio. We cleaned our plates, emptied two bottles of wine, and talked about nothing of consequence until the moon was high in the sky. When Janelle stood, I thought she was heading in, but she locked eyes with me and stripped out of her clothes as I watched.

"Come on," she whispered, raking her gaze over me. She sauntered to the hot tub through the darkness, and I couldn't get my clothes off fast enough.

I don't know how long we stayed in the hot water touching, kissing, exploring each other's bodies like nothing else existed. For me, in those moments, nothing did. It was just Janelle, her soft skin, and her muffled moans against my neck as I made her come with my fingers and later—after I sat her on the tiled edge and watched her nipples harden in the cool night air—my mouth.

Her eyes were heavy when I brought her back to the bedroom, but I kissed her and touched her until she was begging to feel me inside. I stretched out our lovemaking and made her come again and again. I found the angles that made her scream and the ones that stole her breath. I didn't want it to end. I don't want tomorrow to come.

Now she's asleep in my arms and it feels so good I want to kick myself for every night I spent in this house without her next to me.

I was so angry she didn't tell me about Tom's call, but I have to take some responsibility for that. With a few brief exceptions, I've spent the last two weeks doing everything I can to keep her at arm's length. I need her to know she can trust me because I don't want to walk away.

I want to make her smile and hear her laughter. I want to keep her safe and learn about every hurt she's ever felt. I want her to feel like she can tell me her mistakes and share what sacrifices she's made to pursue her passion for acting. I want her to tell me her secrets.

"I sold my soul for my career a long time ago."

"What did you do?" I ask my sleeping angel. I brush her hair from her face, needing the feel of her skin against mine to bury the doubt Gormong planted in my mind today. He laid it out for me—how careful the perp has been not to leave a trace, how Tom doesn't come close to fitting that MO. Extraordinary steps were taken to hide evidence, except everywhere Tom is concerned—the semen, which we can all but assume is Tom, and the security footage, which doesn't give any indication that Tom took Jo from the party against her will.

Now Gormong feels like he has to look into the three women, and if I weren't personally involved with one of them, I might agree. *"If this man is being framed, I just have to convince myself they're not behind it."*

I haven't let myself analyze it much, but Courtney's reaction to her abduction has never sat right with me. It might be politically correct to say that everyone grieves differently, but that's not really true. People all go through the same basic steps when faced with a traumatic event and Courtney didn't. I told myself it was because she couldn't remember it, but then she gave that interview and shared details of the case that could have compromised the investigation. She exploited her own abduction for press and personal gain. She's not the first victim to do so, but it still didn't sit right.

Then there was Jo's disappearance and convenient reappearance. The fact that no one saw either woman in the public restroom they claim to have found themselves in when they came to.

I'm really fucking uncomfortable with doubting women who claim to be victims of sexual assault, but there's enough about this case that doesn't add up that if it were just Courtney and Jo, I probably would have questioned their stories a long time ago.

But it's not just those two. Janelle is tied up in this too, and she admitted just last night that she has dark secrets and has done horrible things in the name of her career. "What is it that you did that you're so ashamed of?" I whisper the question into the darkness where it belongs.

I could have asked her tonight. I could have given her a chance to answer, but I refuse to give voice to the question out of a place of doubt. She needs to tell me in her own time, and she will, and we'll get this whole mess figured out.

I close my eyes and breathe her in. I let what I feel for her fill my heart and my mind until there's no more room for doubt. Until nothing else matters but how much I love her.

* * *

"Good morning," Gormong calls when I step into his office the next morning. He arches a brow. "Someone had a good night."

I shove a cup of coffee in his hands. "Shut up and

drink your coffee. Where are we?"

"Still trying to get the hacker to talk. Fucker's lawyer is going to get him out of here with nothing but a slap on the wrist at this rate."

I shrug. "Priorities, though, right?"

A uniformed officer sticks his head into the room. "Could I have you in interview room three, please?" he asks Gormong. "It's important."

"Sure," Gormong says, rising from his chair.

I follow him into a room down the hall. When the door shuts behind us, the officer looks at me nervously before turning to Gormong. "Maybe you and I should speak alone, sir?"

"You can speak freely in front of Watts," Gormong says. "He's been working closely with us on this investigation."

The officer scratches his head. "The guy we brought in yesterday, the hacker? He took the deal, and he's talking. He admitted to hiring the guys to send the letters and other guys to buy the flowers. And we knew he hacked the security footage at Janelle Crane's building, but we've gotten to see it now."

"And?" I ask.

"There's nothing there. No one broke in. He said his job was to make it look like the footage was missing to cover a break-in when there was none."

I shake my head. "That doesn't make sense. Someone got into her apartment. You saw it for yourselves."

The officer's gaze darts nervously between me and Gormong. "His clients also had him manipulate the software on the cameras at the HiLo."

Gormong inclines his chin. "Clients? Plural?"

"Did Tom Comer hire him?" I ask.

The officer shakes his head. "Three women, he said. They thought they were anonymous, and they contacted him through fake email accounts. But he's a hacker and he made sure he knew who he was working with before he took the job. He tracked their IP addresses and kept records. This guy wasn't stupid."

"Three actresses," Gormong says, and the officer nods with a little wince.

"What?" I see it on Gormong's face. He believes what this criminal is selling them. "Of course he doesn't want to turn in the guy who paid him."

"There was no guy," the officer says.

"I know Janelle." I'm trying to stay calm, but my voice sounds to loud in my ears. "The idea that she would do this is simply outrageous. Don't tell me you're buying it."

Gormong's expression tells me everything I need to know, and I stagger back a step. I was prepared for my friend's well-known stubbornness and determination, but what I see there is worse. I could have handled another emotion, but I'm hobbled by his pity.

"Janelle has been defending Tom through all of this," I say. "Why would she do that if she was trying to frame him?"

"So she'd look innocent," Gormong says. "Just like having you stay with her through all this gives her the perfect alibi."

"She didn't ask me to stay. That was my decision," I

say, and Gormong arches a brow. "Don't. Don't look at me like that. You don't know her like I do."

"And how well is that?" he asks. "As well as you knew Cara? Face it. You lose perspective when your heart's involved."

"There's more," the other officer says before I can respond. "We traced the money that paid the hacker."

We both turn to him.

"Where'd it come from?" Gormong asks.

The officer drags in a ragged breath and studies me. "The money came from Janelle Crane."

CHAPTER EIGHTEEN

Janelle

I'M ON THE BACK PATIO when Cade returns. I hop up when I see him, my smile feeling like it stretches from here to Indiana. "You're back."

Last night was good. Beyond good. It was one of those nights that leaves you warm for days after. But Cade doesn't appear to be reveling in the same afterglow I am.

Exhaustion has sapped the color from his face, and with my first step toward him, I can tell he's upset.

"I'm glad you're home," I say. I put my hands into the pockets of my jeans to keep myself from going to him. "We should talk."

"Do you have a savings account at Washington North Financial?" he asks.

What does that have to do with anything? "Yeah. Why?"

He swallows hard. "And you're doing the *Roommates* movie?"

I can't figure out his mood. What's going on? What does the movie have to do with anything? "Yeah. Didn't we already talk about this? I actually think it's a really great opportunity."

"Or is it the opportunity you wanted all along?"

"Why are we talking about this?" My stomach knots. I'm trying to make the best of a bad situation, but if I had my way, I'd be preparing for my role as Trista, not doing some reprise of a tired, ditzy role. I don't understand why he's suddenly so invested in my career decisions.

"You are so smart. I knew that about you. So fucking smart." He stalks toward me and slips his hand into my hair before tilting my face up to his. His kiss is gentle and he lingers with his lips a breath from mine, his forehead against mine. "You can tell me the truth? Tell me so I know what needs to be done to save you."

"What are you talking about?"

"They found the hacker, princess." He steps back with a heavy sigh. "They found him and he's talking. Gormong is going to be here any minute. Just tell me the truth."

I shake my head. "I don't know what you're talking about. What hacker?"

"The one you hired to frame Tom for abducting and raping Jo and Courtney." He grimaces, as if just saying it is hard for him, but the words don't make any sense. *He's* not making any sense.

"I don't know anything about a hacker."

"Don't lie to me," he says through his teeth. His face contorts as if it's being pulled between frustration and agony. "We can get through this, but not if you lie to me."

"I'm not lying. I don't know what you're talking about." I step forward and press a hand to his chest, as if proximity alone might help me make sense of his words.

He steps away and my hand falls. His Adam's apple bobs as he swallows. "It's funny. I thought I was helping you through one of the hardest, scariest times of your life, but having me here, leading me to believe I was protecting you when I was really just the perfect alibi until you could get revenge and a new movie all in one fell swoop."

This is like one of those dreams where you're walking along and suddenly, out of nowhere, you start falling. That's me right now. Falling. Trying to find footing in this conversation and flailing in midair.

"Gormong's right," Cade says. "I lose my perspective when my heart's involved. That's why I didn't want to fall in love with you."

There's a reckless domino of movement between my chest and stomach at those words. My heart seems to squeeze and fall at the same time as my stomach pitches upward and turns over. Because he's telling me what I want to hear—that he loves me—but he looks broken by the words. Like he hates himself for saying them. And yet I can't hold mine back any longer. I stumble forward, grabbing his shirt as the words stumble out. "I love you too."

He presses his mouth to mine in a kiss that's hard and rough and angry. I cling to his chest, not wanting to let him go and not understanding what's gotten into him.

When he breaks the kiss, he releases me and backs away as if I'm dangerous. "I let myself believe you were different. I would have given you anything. If you would have told me the truth, I would have stood by you through this."

"Different than what?" But his words are starting to click into place in my head. *Hacker you hired. Framing Tom.* "You're confusing me. What happened?"

His eyes lock on something over my shoulder, and he backs away another step. "Goodbye, princess."

Behind me, someone clears his throat, and when I turn Officer Gormong heads toward me with a pair of handcuffs. "Janelle Crane," he says, taking my hands in his, "you have the right to remain silent."

* * *

Cade

I hadn't let myself think about how this thing with Janelle would end, but I never expected I'd have to watch Gormong cuff the woman I love.

I watch his car disappear into the distance and head back into Nate's house. I'm alone—I told Davis and Jamaal to leave before I talked to Janelle—and now I go for the whiskey, fully intending to drink until the alcohol numbs all the terrible shit that's happening in my chest right now.

I pour myself a shot, relishing the burn as it goes down my throat. Janelle used me. She lied to me. And she hurt me. But the only person I hate right now is myself. I hate myself for being such a damn fool. For believing her. For never suspecting, even a little, that she might be capable of this. For wanting to get to her before the police and tell her she'd been found out, to help her run.

But mostly, I hate myself for the hurt in her eyes when Officer Gormong cuffed her. That's what I think about when I throw back the second shot, and the third.

Cara's betrayal is an old wound that never seemed to heal, and when they put the evidence in my face at the station—the payment info from Janelle's accounts, the IP addresses that match each of the girls' locations—I wasn't just angry with Janelle, I was angry with myself for being duped. For believing we had a connection. For being so oblivious to a deception of this magnitude.

I'll admit, I was beginning to believe that the other two women might be behind all this, but never Janelle. Fuck, I still don't believe it, even after I've seen the evidence with my own eyes and talked to the guy she hired.

"Three women. Obviously friends. They'd been planning this for months."

I can't wrap my brain around it. Janelle is a good actress, and she's been hurt by Tom, but I never would have believed she'd be capable of framing him for something so heinous. Did I only see what I wanted to see?

I pour another shot. Maybe I'll drink until I pass out so I don't have these images of her smiling face flashing through my mind. Was it all a lie? Just like Cara? Was I nothing more than an alibi for her?

I love you too.

I down another shot and then press my palms to my temples. Maybe she's lying to protect me. Maybe she got in too deep and didn't know how to get out.

I yank my phone from my pocket and dial Gormong. He answers on the first ring.

"Take care of her," I say quickly, faintly aware that my words are slurring together. "If she did this, she had a reason. Maybe the other two blackmailed her or maybe—"

"Go back home to Indiana, Cade. We'll take care of this."

"Listen to me." My voice cracks and I swear I feel it split right down through my chest. "She's special. She's a *good* person."

His sigh fills the line. "Don't do this to yourself, man."

"Fuck, just . . . Just make sure she has a good lawyer."

"She'll need one."

* * *

Janelle

I've been in this room before. The bare walls and cold metal chairs are familiar. Only, the last time I was here, I was worried about my friend and scared for my own safety. This time I'm being accused of conspiring to frame a man for rape.

The hacker that was behind the missing footage at my condo was also the man who arranged to have the flowers sent to us. He's the man who made sure the security cameras at the HiLo never saw Courtney leave. They have evidence that Jo, Courtney, and I communicated with him from our home computers. And he was paid with money from *my* savings account. It's an account I opened with my inheritance after my father died and never touched. I didn't want that money. And now it's gone. Used to pay a man to coordinate this whole ordeal.

I've been in police custody for six hours and I've already seen my lawyer. She says this doesn't look good for me. She doesn't believe me. I could see it in her eyes. She thinks I'm lying. Officer Gormong thinks I'm lying. I'm legitimately at risk of going to prison for a crime I didn't commit, and I'm scared.

But that fear is nothing compared to the pain in my heart.

I don't blame the police for not believing me. I don't blame my lawyer. But *Cade* thinks I did this.

Cade thinks I would frame my ex-husband for rape. *Cade* believes I'd do the worst, all to revive my career.

I can't say he didn't warn me. He told me he doesn't

trust actresses. But was it so foolish of me to believe I was different? To believe that loving me meant he could trust me?

I'm haunted by my own words to Tom. I told him that forgiveness and trust weren't the same thing. Apparently, neither are love and trust. To Cade, I will always be part of the Hollywood machine he detests so much, and that makes him incapable of trusting me.

The door clicks open and I don't even look up. I've been questioned again and again, and it's always the same. They've asked me the same dozen questions in forty different ways. My lawyer suggested I stop answering when she's not present, and since I'm paying her a small fortune for that bit of advice, I've decided to take it. This time I won't talk.

Someone passes a cup of coffee across the table to me.

"In case you need this as much as I do." The voice is so sweet to my ears, and I lift my head as Cade takes the seat across from me.

His dark eyes are all over me, taking in my eyes, my mouth, then lingering on my cuffed hands resting on the table.

My heart doubles its pace and seems to be whispering, *He came. He came.*

"I'm going to get you out of here. We'll get you the best lawyer in town. After what Tom put you through, any jury would understand—"

"You still believe I did this?" Any hope I felt when he walked in the door melts away.

He flinches and drops his gaze to the table. "You

told me. Don't you remember?"

I don't bother replying. This has to be a bad dream. All this evidence against me and now Cade's saying I confessed the crime to him? This is a nightmare.

So then why does the hurt in my heart feel so real?

"You told me you sold your soul for your career. You told me that hiring Matthew wasn't close to the worst thing you'd done." He lifts his gaze to mine, and his face is a map of conflicting emotions. "I love you, and I'm going to stick by you. I'm going to get you through this."

I didn't think the ache in my heart could grow, but it does, and I press my palm to my chest as if the pressure might fuse its pieces back together. "I was talking about the beginning of my career," I whisper. "I was talking about the time I walked in on my husband fucking the casting producer of *Roommates*. She was married, but she was fucking my husband, and I pretended not to know what happened."

"Janelle," Cade whispers. "I didn't know."

Hot tears spill down my cheeks, but I don't wipe them away. I'm not going to hide my heartbreak from Cade. He broke me, and he now he has to face that. "I confronted Tom later, and he told me he did it for me. It was screwed up and twisted, but Tom had fucked that woman in exchange for the promise that I'd get that role, and if she found out that I knew, I wouldn't get the part. He loved me. He was sorry. It was horrible, but my happiness was more important than anything, and he knew how much I wanted that chance. I was young, and I was stupid and desperate for a real break, and I kept my mouth shut and told myself he was telling the truth, told myself he'd done it for me." I swallow hard. "My marriage was never the same. And neither was my confidence. I couldn't get a role with my talent alone. The betrayal wasn't just in that my husband would so easily fuck another woman. It was in that he didn't believe I was good enough to get the part on my own."

"Why didn't you tell me?" He reaches across the table for my hands, but I pull them away, dropping them to my lap. I can't endure his touch right now.

"Tom may have been the one who fucked her, but staying silent made *me* the whore. Don't you see why I couldn't tell you yet? I wanted you to believe in me before I showed you that part of myself." I scoot my chair back and stand. "But you're no better than Tom. You don't believe in me, and you never will. Cara wounded you too deeply, and any feelings you have for me will always be cast in the shadow of *her* betrayal. I deserve better than that."

"I'm sorry." He clenches his fists on the table. "But don't shut me out right now. I will fight to get you out of here and get your name cleared."

"I don't want your help," I whisper. "And I don't want to see you again."

Slowly, he pushes his chair back, and the metal screeches against the tile floor. "I'm sorry," he whispers again. "I'm so fucking sorry."

I press my palm to my chest again. It doesn't help, but when something hurts that badly, my instinct is to try. "Leave."

CHAPTER NINETEEN

Cade

My head is going to split into two. I used the last of the favors I had to get a chance to talk to Janelle yesterday, and when she told me to get out, I came back to her brother's mansion and drank.

No amount of alcohol could numb the ache in my chest or erase the knowledge that I fucked up, but that didn't keep me from trying, and I'm paying for it this morning with a hangover from hell.

She's innocent and I didn't believe in her. It doesn't make sense in light of the evidence, but I know it's the truth, and I'm a fucking idiot for getting myself in this condition because I need my brain clear now more than ever. She wants me out of her life, but before I leave I need to figure out how to prove she's innocent.

I stumble to the kitchen and fill a glass from the tap. The idea of water is nauseating, but it's the only thing that will lessen the pounding in my head.

I stop the cup halfway to my lips as my mind fills

with an image—Courtney, Jo, and Bella, raising their glasses in a toast. *"May he get what's coming to him."*

"Bella even bought a condo in the same building as Janelle."

"Three women. Obviously friends. They'd been planning this for months."

Fuck.

I find my phone on the counter and dial Gormong. "It wasn't Janelle."

"Cade—"

"The third woman was Bella Comer, Comer's second wife. She has a condo in Janelle's building. I bet you anything she was accessing Janelle's condo and computer from her own to make it look like Janelle was the third. And once she was in Janelle's condo, I bet she found everything she needed to access Janelle's account. Tom Comer isn't the only one who was framed."

* * *

Janelle

I click off the TV and my sister-in-law spins around and scowls at me. "I was watching that."

"They don't deserve any more of your attention or mine," I say, propping my hands on my hips.

She holds up a finger. "They slept with your husband while you were still married to him." She adds

LEXI RYAN

a second finger. "They tried to implicate you in a crime you didn't commit." And a third. "And they're kind of just all-around bitchy women. You cannot blame me for wanting to watch their asses be hauled off to jail."

"*Prison*," I say.

She shrugs. "Even better. But I was enjoying the show. I only wish they hadn't offered them the plea deal. I wanted to see the three of them turn on each other in court. *That* would have been entertainment."

"Screw entertainment." I settle onto the couch and draw up my knees. "I just want the whole thing behind me."

She plops into the chair beside me. "You're sure you can't stay for another day or two?"

I absolutely could. There's nothing but pride sending me back to LA, but every day I'm here, I worry I'll run into Cade. "I'm not ready to see him yet," I admit, swallowing. "I think it would hurt too much."

"Have you talked to him since . . .?"

"Since I compared him to my POS ex-husband and told him I didn't want him in my life?"

Hanna flinches. "It sounds so bad when you put it that way."

I shake my head. "What's there to say?"

"I don't know. What about telling him that you love him so much you're a mess and, hey, by the way, *thanks for figuring out that Bella was behind all of this and keeping me from serving hard time*."

I bite my lip. It's been a month and a half, but I still can't talk about Cade without my throat getting thick and tears pricking at the back of my eyes. "He thought I was capable of setting someone up for rape just to further my career."

"For a minute he did," Hanna says, her big brown eyes searching mine. "And I know that's terrible, but he was also willing to stay by your side even if you were guilty. Crap on a cracker, Elle, that's about the most romantic thing I've ever heard, and that's not even counting the part where he came to his senses and saved the day. If he'd *really* believed you were capable of that, his mind wouldn't have been searching for an explanation."

"I know," I whisper. "And I can't blame him for thinking I was part of it. Even for a minute. But at the end of the day, I'm still an actress, and he's still a man who hates my city more than anything."

"Why can't New Hope be your city?"

I sigh. "Because I'm the foolish optimist who still believes she can live out her dream of playing important parts in important movies. Maybe someday I'll give up the dream, but I'm not ready yet."

Absently, Hanna rubs her belly. "I just hate seeing you so sad."

"I'm fine." And it's kind of true. Even if my heart is broken, I'm grateful for Cade. After being loved in such a sincere and healthy way, I couldn't go back to the kind of relationship I had with Tom. I owe Cade for that. But I miss him so much that sometimes I wake up in the middle of the night and the ache in my chest is so intense, all I can do is curl into a ball and pray the pain passes. It never does, but some moments it's more unbearable than others.

Hanna's phone buzzes with her text alert. She picks it up and frowns at it.

"What is it?" I ask.

"Liz just sent me a link. She says, 'Is this true?'" She taps her phone, clicking on the link, and her jaw drops. "*Actress Janelle Crane secretly expecting hunky cop lover's baby.*" Her eyes snap up to mine. "This isn't true, is it?"

My stomach plummets as I snag the phone from her and read the short article. It claims a "reliable source close to the actress" reported that I'm newly pregnant. "Oh no," I whisper. "Cade's going to hate this." I swear, I have the worst luck with this man.

"Is it true?"

I glare at her. "Of course not. It's bullshit. Clearly it's a slow news day and they're just making shit up now."

Hanna frowns at my stomach. "That's too bad. I bet a baby would make Cade grovel appropriately." Her eyes fly to mine. "Oh my God. Does *he* know you're not pregnant?"

"Of course he—" I look at the article again. "I mean, he should— Crap." I hand Hanna back her phone and grab for mine, dialing Cade for the first time since before I was arrested.

The call goes straight to voicemail and his no-nonsense message. "You've reached Cade. Leave a message." It beeps, and I sit silently for a beat before punching the screen to end the call.

"He didn't answer?" Hanna asks.

"It went straight to voicemail. I didn't want to talk

about this to a recording." Or maybe I just want to hear his voice for real and not some canned recording.

She frowns at my phone, as if it's responsible for Cade not answering. "That's understandable."

I tap my screen to dial him again. "I'll just tell him to call me."

His voicemail picks up, and I hang up again.

"What now?" Hanna asks.

"What if it's going straight to voicemail because he's screening his calls?"

"You really think he's going to send your call to voicemail once he reads *this*?" she asks, holding up her phone. "Have some faith in the man."

"Right." I dial again, feeling another little piece of my heart break off at the sound of his voice in the short message. It beeps and Hanna waves her hand at me in an *out with it* gesture. "Cade." I clear my throat. "This is Janelle. I, um, I'm sorry to bother you. Could you call me, please? We need to talk."

I hang up, then look desperately to Hanna. "Did that sound like I needed to tell him I'm pregnant? Crap. What if—"

"Relax." She looks way too pleased. "He'll call. You'll talk. It'll be good."

"Statistically, you're oh for one on predictions about Cade," I tell her. "But I hope you're right about this one."

* * *

Janelle

He hates me even more than I thought. It's the only explanation for why he wouldn't have called me back in the twenty-four hours since I left the first message.

I canceled my flight yesterday, deciding I should stay in New Hope to have this conversation with Cade face to face.

Only he's not even returning my calls, and I'm too chicken to go to his apartment, so I'm not sure I'm going to get that opportunity.

"Now I'm mad at him," Hanna says.

We're sitting at Brady's, and I'm nursing a beer while she drinks a "vodka cranberry, hold the vodka," because she's adorable like that.

"You've been mad at him since you found out he watched them cuff me and read me my rights."

"I was *unhappy* before," she says. "Now I'm *mad*. I mean, if you're having his baby, he should be here, talking it out, figuring what happens next and how you're going to make it work."

"Maybe he doesn't want to make it work," I point out.

She scoffs. "Then he's an idiot."

"Lower your voice," I whisper.

She sits up straighter. "What's that? You want me to say it louder?" She stands up and clears her throat. "Cade Watts is an idiot."

"Yeah," adds a familiar deep voice. "He definitely is."

I look up, and there's Cade.

Hanna spins around, and her cheeks flame red, but she lifts her chin. "You are."

He nods to me. "Could I talk to Janelle alone for a minute?"

"It's about time," Hanna mutters, but she winks at me as she grabs her purse and exits the booth.

Cade takes her spot. He looks amazing. Somehow, he's even broader and taller than I remember. His hair's longer than it was when I saw him last, and I want to run my fingers through where it's just starting to curl at the back of his neck. Just seeing those arms makes my stomach twist into knots with how badly I want him to hold me.

In the movie, this is where the hero grovels and holds the heroine. He kisses her and tells her he's been a damn fool. But this isn't a movie. It's my life. And I owe Cade the apology, not the other way around.

"I've been trying to call you," I say, scanning his face for any hint as to how angry he is or how much he hates me now. I don't want him to hate me. Even if we can't be together.

"I've been out of town." He folds his hands on the table, and his gaze drops to my beer. For a moment, I get a flash of emotion across his face, but it's gone before I can read it.

"Where were you?"

"I flew to LA." He swallows and slowly lifts his gaze to meet mine. "As soon as I saw the article."

I shake my head, and my eyes burn with tears I only wish I could hide from him. The last thing I want is for him to feel emotionally manipulated into comforting me. "It's not true. I have no idea who their source is or why anyone would say such a thing."

"I'm sorry to hear that," he says.

"I called the paper and I asked them to print a retraction and— What? What are you sorry about?"

He lifts a shoulder in an awkward half-shrug and his gaze drops to the table, as if he can see my stomach through the wood. "I may have jumped the gun and put in some calls about jobs out there."

Everything from my chest to my belly seems to melt, one inch at a time. "You were looking for jobs in LA?"

Another shrug. "I wasn't planning on freeloading off the mother of my child, if that's what you're asking."

"You would have moved to LA if I'd been pregnant?"

"You wouldn't have to be pregnant." Finally, *finally* he touches me. He reaches across the table and grazes the back of my hand with his fingers. The move is tentative and vulnerability is written across his face, but the contact might as well be my lifeline. "I'd move there just to be with you. If you'd have me."

"You hate LA."

"I hated my memories there." He lifts my hand to take it into his. "But I have some new memories now, and I'd like to make more."

"I've missed you," I whisper.

"It's been hell," he says.

My phone clatters against the table as it buzzes with

a text. My gaze catches on Matt Hailey's name flashing across the screen, and I read the text.

I know you didn't want my help anymore, but I couldn't resist. Hoping the article brought you and your beau back together.

"Damn you, Matt," I mutter.

Cade takes the phone to read the message and smiles. "Occasionally that guy makes a good decision." He lifts his eyes to mine. "Tell me what you're thinking."

I shake my head, unsure where to start. "That it wasn't fair of me to compare you to Tom. You're nothing like him. And that I shouldn't have pushed you away when you really wanted to help me."

"I fucked up," he whispers. "And I've been paying the price. I love you so much that every day apart from you hurts more than the last. That 'time heals' crap is just bullshit. This isn't getting any better. I love you and I need you, and I do believe in you. So much that I want to be with you in LA when you finally get to play the kind of part you want so badly."

My breath catches and I have to swallow hard to clear the thickness from my throat so I can speak. "At this moment, this is the only part I want to play."

"What part is that?"

"The part where the woman is given another chance with the man she loves."

"That's a favorite of mine." He leads me out of the booth and stands before me, my hands in his. "Please tell me this is where the idiot guy is forgiven and gets to kiss the beautiful girl."

I nod. And he does.

EPILOGUE

Cade
Three months later . . .

My steps echo through the foyer as I pace. The sound does nothing to soothe my nerves. "Janelle," I call up the stairs. "The car is here." I open the front door and signal the driver that we'll be a couple of minutes. I need to talk to Janelle before we can go.

Jesus. These nerves. My stomach's in knots and there's a slight tremble to my hands. I've never been this nervous. Then again, nothing has ever mattered this much.

"How do I look?"

Turning, I watch my girlfriend descend the stairs, and I have to swallow hard. After three months of living together in her brother's Hollywood mansion, her effect on me hasn't changed. If anything, she's more beautiful to me now than ever. Every day exposes another layer of her beauty—her loyalty to her family, her love for her nieces and nephew, her sass and wit and quirky sense of humor.

The sight of her calms me, and I draw in what feels

like my first full breath of the evening.

"Well?" She takes the last few steps and comes to stand in front of me. "Do I look like a respectable actress?"

I pretend to consider her question. Her hair is pinned into a twist at the back of her head, and her floor-length black dress has a slit up the side that reaches the top of her thigh. My hands itch to slide under it. I already know the sounds she'll make when I graze my knuckles down the center of her panties, but like an addict I want to hear them again. As soon as fucking possible.

She clears her throat. "You keep looking at me like that, and we'll be late to meet Helen."

Shrugging, I close the space between us. "We should make her wait. She deserves the torment."

Helen Kerensky is taking us to dinner to grovel. She asked Janelle to take the role of Trista after all, and Janelle's making her sweat before she accepts. Janelle's agent said Helen can't find anyone else who can pull off the emotionally complex role, and she's offering a new, better contract. Apparently the producer values her art over her pride.

"You look beautiful," I say softly. A small smile curves her pink lips, and I have to shove my hands into my pockets to keep myself from kissing her.

"I'm excited. Helen's a bit temperamental, but she's a genius. I can't wait for you to meet her."

I love seeing her this happy. She's practically vibrated with nerves and excitement since she found out the part of Trista was hers for the taking. She's been walking around with the aura of a woman who's not just watching her dreams unfold, but who is in full control of how it will happen.

"Tonight, you'll tell her you accept?"

She grins. "Yeah. I'm ready. This is going to be the biggest challenge of my career."

"Your life is going to change." My voice cracks on the words, my nerves showing despite my efforts to hide them. "You know that, right?"

She takes my tie in her hand and tugs, pulling me another step closer. "I hope some things will stay the same." Her gaze drops to my lips, and when I don't kiss her, she releases my tie. "I won't let my career change you and me. Okay? This is too important."

In my pocket, my fingers brush against velvet and my heart kicks up a beat. "What if I want things between us to change?" She flinches, but before she can speak, I drop to a knee and pull the jewelry box from my pocket, opening it so she can see the ring inside.

"Cade, what . . .?" Her eyes widen and fill with tears. "Oh . . ."

"Janelle Crane," I say around the thickness in my throat, "your dreams are coming true, and you deserve them all." I bring her hand to my lips and kiss her knuckles. "You're truly the most amazing woman I've ever known, and the last three months have been better than anything I could have imagined. Tonight marks the beginning of the life you've wanted for so long, and no matter how your life changes, I want to be part of it. You already have my heart. Now I want you to have this ring. Will you marry me?"

Her lips part and she drags in a ragged breath.

"You're wrong," she whispers, sinking to her knees in front of me. "The life I've wanted started the second you came back to me."

"Is that an answer?"

She blinks away tears and giggles. "Yes. Of course I'll marry you."

Something washes over me—bigger than relief and more than love. *Gratitude.* For her. For this life. For second and third chances. I take the ring from the box and slide it onto her finger.

"Where did you get this?" she asks.

"I spent a month visiting every jewelry store in the city trying to find the perfect ring, and I couldn't find anything that felt special enough. Last week, when I met with your brother to get his blessing—"

"You got Nate's blessing?"

"Well, yeah. I like my balls and figured he'd cut them off if I didn't." She laughs and I grin. *Fuck,* she makes me happy. "He gave me the ring. He said it was your grandmother's."

She nods and a tear slips down her cheek as she studies the vintage piece—a French-cut diamond set in white gold and framed by three small pearls. "I didn't know what happened to it. It's perfect."

"It looks beautiful on you."

She lifts her eyes to meet mine. "You're really going to marry an actress? A spoiled Hollywood princess?"

"I'm going to marry *you*, and you might be a fucking fantastic actress, but you're a lot more to me than that. You're my friend, my lover . . ." I slide a hand into her hair and brush my thumb across her cheek. "The future mother of my children."

She draws in a ragged breath. "Cade . . ."

"No rush on the last one. I understand your career comes first right now."

She shakes her head. "I can't wait to have your babies. I'm just not sure there's room for any more joy in my chest right now. You're amazing. I love you so much."

"I love you too. Forever."

When I press my mouth to hers, she loosens my tie and unbuttons my shirt.

"We're going to be late," I murmur against her mouth.

My future wife just grins, unzips her dress, and lets it fall to the floor. "Is that a promise?"

THE END

Thank you for reading *Holding Her Close,* the second book in the Mended Hearts series. If you'd like to receive an email when I release a new book, please visit my website to sign up for my newsletter.

HOLDING HER CLOSE
PLAYLIST

"Same Old Love" by Selena Gomez
"Something Better" by Audien, Lady Antebellum
"Oblivion" by Bastille
"Ghost" by Halsey
"Fallingforyou" by The 1975
"Say You Love Me" by Jessie Ware
"Believe" by Mumford & Sons
"Nothing Without Love" by Nate Ruess

ACKNOWLEDGMENTS

I owe huge thanks to my family for all their support. Brian, thank you for understanding my dream, for answering plot questions, and for believing in me when I don't believe in myself. Jack and Mary, thank you for making me laugh and giving me a reason to work hard. I am so proud to be your mommy. To my sister Kim, for watching the kids and giving my husband and I much-needed date nights and for pimping my books to all her friends. Thanks to my mom, who checks on me when I'm putting in too many hours, who reminds me to take care of myself but is always careful not to nag.

I have so much gratitude for my friends. You encourage me, you believe in me, and you remind me not to take myself too seriously. A special shout-out to Mira, whose calls save me from meltdowns; to Kylie, who introduced me to barbells and gave me a healthy new obsession; to my new neighbors, Amy, Amber, Tammy, and Sarah, who made me feel so welcome when we moved in; and to Justin, who answers almost as many book-related hypothetical questions as my husband and is the most dedicated Rick Roller I've ever met.

To everyone who provided me feedback on Janelle's story along the way—especially Heather Carver, Dina Littner, and Samantha Leighton—you're all awesome. To Lexi's Midnight Readers, who inspire me daily with their love for all things New Hope.

Thank you to the team that helped me package this book and promote it. Sarah Hansen at Okay Creations designed my beautiful cover. You may have noticed I'm partial to her work, and will keep her on my team as long as she'll let me. Lauren McKellar, thank you for the insightful line edits. Thanks to Arran McNicol at Editing720 for proofreading, and my new PA, Lisa, who posts all those pictures of gorgeous men on my Facebook page—a dirty job, but somebody's gotta do it. A shout-out to all of the bloggers and reviewers who help spread the word about my books. I am humbled by the time you take out of your busy lives for my stories. You're the best.

To my agent, Dan Mandel, and my foreign rights agent, Stefanie Diaz, for getting my books into the hands of readers all over the world. Thank you for being part of my team.

To my NWBs—Sawyer Bennett, Lauren Blakely, Violet Duke, Jessie Evans, Melody Grace, Monica Murphy, and Kendall Ryan—y'all rock my world. I'm inspired by your tireless work and always encouraged by your friendship. Thank you for being a part of this journey.

To all my writer friends on Twitter, Facebook, and my various writer loops—especially to the Fast Draft Club and the All Awesome group—thank you for keeping me company during those fourteen-hour work days.

And last but certainly not least, a big thank-you to my fans—the coolest, smartest, best readers in the world. I owe my career to you. You're the reason I get to do this every day and the reason I *want* to. I appreciate each and every one of you. You're the best!

~Lexi

LOVE UNBOUND
BY LEXI RYAN

If you enjoyed *Holding Her Close*, you may also enjoy the other books in Love Unbound, the linked series of books set in New Hope and about the characters readers have come to love.

Splintered Hearts (A Love Unbound Series)
Unbreak Me (Maggie's story)
Stolen Wishes: A Wish I May Prequel Novella (Will and Cally's prequel)
Wish I May (Will and Cally's novel)
Or read them together in the omnibus edition,
Splintered Hearts: The New Hope Trilogy

Here and Now (A Love Unbound Series)
Lost in Me (Hanna's story begins)
Fall to You (Hanna's story continues)
All for This (Hanna's story concludes)
Or read them together in the omnibus edition, *Here and Now: The Complete Series*

Reckless and Real (A Love Unbound Series)
Something Wild (Liz and Sam's story begins)
Something Reckless (Liz and Sam's story continues)
Something Real (Liz and Sam's story concludes)
Or read them together in the omnibus edition, *Reckless and Real: The Complete Series*

Mended Hearts (A Love Unbound Series)
Playing with Fire (Nix's story)

HOLDING HER CLOSE

Holding Her Close (Janelle and Cade's story)

Other Titles by Lexi Ryan

Hot Contemporary Romance
Text Appeal
Accidental Sex Goddess

Decadence Creek Stories and Novellas
Just One Night
Just the Way You Are

CONTACT

I love hearing from readers, so find me on my Facebook page at facebook.com/lexiryanauthor, follow me on Twitter @writerlexiryan, shoot me an email at writerlexiryan@gmail.com, or find me on my website: www.lexiryan.com.